Running

To Save America

Robert, you have been so good to our family and we appreciate it so much. May God continue to bless you.

Don Flanders

DON FLANDERS

ISBN-13: 9780615906591
ISBN-10: 0615906591

Introduction

"Running"...some fact and some fiction... life as it was...life as it could have been... life as it should have been...if only a few decisions had been made differently...if a few events had turned out differently. It is the story of Dan Fleming, white, and Ben West, black, born in 1943. They grew up in segregated government housing projects in Savannah, Georgia. They became best friends as young children but were separated at nine years of age, thinking they would never see each other again. However, their paths cross as teens and in college, and they remain best friends for life. Both of them were superior athletes hoping for professional careers. Each suffered serious injuries that ended those hopes at an early age.

Achieving success in their chosen business careers, they both end up in Chattanooga, Tennessee as young men. Ben, a black conservative, is elected to Congress in 1990 with Dan as his most trusted advisor. While Dan is helping his friend in Congress, he is surprised to learn that a family secret his father had shared with him many years ago is revealed with more clarity. It is a story linking Dan's uncle's murder to the assassination of President Kennedy, and it now impacts the future of our country. Together they find a way to set our country back on a Constitutional path that would eliminate our huge debt, preserving America for our children and grandchildren.

Prologue

It was June, 1964. I had just returned from the University of Georgia after my junior year to my home in Savannah. I would begin my summer job at the National Paper Company in five days. Dad was 70 years old now, recovering very well from a heart attack at 65 years of age. I asked him if he wanted to go fishing for a couple of days at Middleton's Lake, one of our favorite fishing spots over the years. We borrowed my brother's truck and camping gear and headed out early Wednesday morning.

We had a good day of fishing and talking. Dad loved to tell stories of yesteryear, about the trouble he and his five brothers got into while growing up on the family's 1200 acre farm. I laughed at each story. They truly were funny...and that pleased him. As I set the tent that night and built a small fire, Dad put the fish on ice.

We sat down to a dinner of scrambled eggs, crisp bacon and pan fried biscuits, Dad still talking. I interjected, "Dad, I love to hear you tell those stories, but don't you think that you should slow down before we try to go to sleep?"

"You're right, Dan," he said. "But I have one more tale I want you to hear…one I've never told to anyone. You're my best listener, so I want you to hear it first…before I die." That got my attention. He smeared some strawberry preserves that Mom had made on a biscuit and began. "The year was 1910. I was 16 years old. The family farm at that time was 360 acres of good land… rolling hills, lots of good timber and good water. Hunting was great…plenty of deer, boar and birds of all kinds."

He continued, "It was the end of October. The cotton was picked and sent to the gin, so my brothers and I went to our winter jobs. Your Uncle Perry and I would be cutting timber and hauling it to the saw mills in the area. Your Uncle Jake could fix anything that was broken or wearing out, so that was his responsibility over the winter months. Your Uncle Fed, the oldest at 30, had a plum of a job over the winter. He worked for an exclusive hunting lodge on Jekyll Island. At the time the island was owned by J.P. Morgan, one of the wealthiest men in the world…a big New York banker. He built this beautiful and expensive lodge on Jekyll and allowed his rich friends from all over the world to come there to escape the cold North and do a little hunting and fishing. Your Uncle Fed was paid well by the club and he always got big tips from those rich guys. You know what a legend he was around here with a rifle, pistol and a shotgun. Well, Fed would put on shooting displays for these wealthy men and they loved it…trusted him to lead them on a hunt."

"Yeeaa," I said, "I always liked being at a dove shoot with Uncle Fed, watching him bring down two doves with one shot, as the doves crossed in flight. Few people can do that. Incidentally, Dad, why do we call him Fed when his name is Fred?"

"Two of the brothers had trouble pronouncing their "r's," so they called him Fed…the name stuck," Dad chuckled.

Dad took a sip of iced tea and continued, "Dave Wiseman, the club's manager, called Fed into his office on November 18th…told him that a group of very important men were coming to the club next week for a week of business planning, and to do a little hunting. It was a secret meeting, so all of the regular help except him and Fed were given the week off so there wouldn't be much talk about this event. Replacement help was brought in from the mainland, paid well and told to keep quiet. Fed was told to keep quiet about this group or he would lose his job. The seven well-dressed men arrived in a private railcar at the Brunswick railroad station and were quickly ferried across to Jekyll Island to the lodge."

"The first two days the men were up early and dressed for business. Fed said that they were holed up in the conference room behind closed doors all day…until nearly midnight… coming out only for meals and to relieve themselves. On the third morning Fed took them duck hunting as had been scheduled. He recognized Senator Aldrich and big New York bank owners Benjamin Strong and Henry Davison who were partners of J.P. Morgan. They had been to the club a few times in the past. He had taken them on a few hunts and found them friendly enough. Fed tried to strike up a conversation with them, but none of them cared to talk much. Senator Aldrich commented on Fed's hunting skills and what a crack shot he was. Nothing else was said. They were back at the lodge for the noon meal, spending the remainder of the day behind closed doors until late at night."

"On the fourth day the weather turned much colder. The group said that they weren't going to stand in knee-deep marsh water waiting for a duck to fly over, freezing while wet and cold. They declined to go duck hunting again. Fed told them that there was plenty of deer and boar on the south end of the island if they didn't mind walking a couple of miles….not much interest from them. Then he asked if any of them had ever been quail hunting. None of them had been, so Fed told them about the sport…the excitement of the bird dogs…the beauty of watching the dogs in the act of finding and pointing out a covey of quail…the birds in scattered flight…the dogs fetching the downed birds and bringing them back to the shooter. He told them of our farm nearby, loaded with quail. What fun it would be. They went for it. Fed came over to the house that afternoon and arranged the hunt with Papa. We would start early in the morning two days later."

"That night it turned even colder so Fed went over to the pot bellied wood stove against the wall and opened the door to the stove to start a fire. There was plenty of wood in the corner of the room. Upon opening the door, he could hear voices coming out of the stove. It was a conversation in the meeting room that he was hearing. Fed recognized some of the voices. The stove's flue was tied into a common chimney which ran from the bottom floor to the top floor. Fed's room was on the third floor directly above the meeting room. When he opened the door to the stove he could hear every word they said, clear as a bell, as the sound travelled up the chimney like an intercom. He listened for over an hour before the men retired for the evening, fascinated at what he heard…the secrecy…not understanding much of it."

"Next morning after handling a few chores, Fed returned to his room and locked the door. He told David Wiseman that he was going to rest today…not feeling well. The truth is, Fed wanted to listen in on this secret meeting all day. Senator Aldrich appeared to be the leader of the group, but the man called Paul seemed to know more about the banking operations which were being discussed. He had a German accent and lectured the others quite often when they questioned his proposals…irritated them. They talked about not calling their operation a central bank, concealing their real intent from the public and from Congress. One of them suggested that they set up a system of regional banks so the public will think that control of their central bank was not centered in New York. These regional banks will have little power but the people won't know that. The more he listened over the next few days and nights, the more he came to believe that these very powerful and wealthy men were up to no good…planning to take over the banking and finance business of the government…controlling the issuance of our currency… setting interest rates on loans...fleecing the people of the country with no thought of how immoral it was. There was so much Fed didn't understand about banking, credit and finance that he couldn't be sure of that, so for the time being he decided to keep his thoughts to himself.

"Two days before the meeting was to end, five of the men went with Fed to our farm for their much anticipated quail hunt. They were excited. The German and Senator Aldrich stayed at the lodge. The group arrived just at daybreak and they were hungry. Mama treated them all to a breakfast of country ham and eggs, biscuits and red eye gravy. They loved it. Each of the men had double-barrel, 12-gauge shotguns from the lodge. Fed and I took three of the men with us and headed toward the timberline while Papa and Perry took the other two in the opposite direction for the river bottom. I was in charge of the dogs, Bing and Sally, two of the fine pointers who were best at finding quail. Fed explained what each man should do once the dogs found a covey of quail and pointed them out. We had a successful morning. The dogs were great and the men proved to be good shots, each bringing down at least two birds."

"Papa and his group were equally successful and were headed back to the house at the agreed upon time. While crossing a barbed-wire fence, Papa pushed the top wire down so everyone could step over the fence. Charles Norton laid his shotgun up against the fence post where Papa stood. As he picked his leg up to straddle the fence, he kicked his shotgun over. The gun slid along the wire, falling sideways until the trigger caught one of the barbs, causing the gun to discharge. Papa yelled and fell to the ground… bloody from his thigh to his armpit as the number eight birdshot tore through his body at close range. Papa took the blast at an angle as the gun was pointed mostly upward. He was badly hurt so we rushed him to our family doctor in Brunswick. Mr. Norton turned white…fearful of the event… nervously talked to the others so we couldn't hear them."

"After the doctor removed the small pellets, he told us that Papa would be fine….no internal organs damaged...just a badly wounded thigh muscle that might cause him a little trouble… might limp a little for the rest of his life. Papa would spend a few nights in the doctor's clinic so he could be cared for properly. Mr. Norton offered to pay the bills. The others went back to the Lodge, but Mr. Norton had to stay and talk to the county sheriff. Any shooting had to be reported to the sheriff and investigated whether it was an accident or not. The sheriff asked Papa if he was going to press charges. Papa told him that was ridiculous…was an accident…and Mr. Norton has agreed to pay all of the medical bills. Mr. Norton pulled Fed to one side and asked him who Papa did his banking with. Fed told him it was Glynn County Bank, down the street a block. Mr. Norton said the he wanted to talk to Papa's banker before he and Fed headed back to the lodge. Mr. Norton spent over an hour with the bank's president behind closed doors. Then he and Fed went back to the lodge to join the rest."

"Next morning Fed continued to listen in on the meeting downstairs. Senator Aldrich spoke angrily to the group…telling them to let him worry about getting the bill through Congress…he knew which Congressmen and Senators he could buy off to get their votes.

"Mr. Davison said that even if they got the bill through Congress, President Taft won't sign it. 'You know how he and his Republicans hate us bankers and the idea of a central bank...in New York. The people won't go for it.' "

"Aldrich spoke up again and told them that they will just have to defeat President Taft in the 1912 election...elect someone who will sign the bill. They will run a third party candidate who can split the Republican vote to get their man elected. Then they will get their Federal Reserve Bill signed into law. Fed told me that he couldn't believe his ears, but that is exactly what they said."

"After the seven men got on their private railcar two days later and headed back to New York, Fed went into Dave Wiseman's office. He asked Dave if he knew what this meeting was all about. Dave said the he didn't know and didn't want to know. Fed told Dave what he had heard and what he thought about it. Dave told him that he should keep all of those thoughts to himself...could be a lot of trouble for you if you don't. Fed wouldn't be hired back at the lodge next season...or ever."

"Two weeks later Papa's banker saw Mama in town where she was doing a little shopping, and asked her to tell Papa to stop by his office as soon as he could. "It's important," he told her. Papa, still limping, slowly walked into his office late that afternoon. The banker told Papa that Mr. Norton was president of one of the biggest banks in the country, a wealthy and powerful man. "Here's a letter from Mr. Norton to you, telling you how sorry he was to have caused you so much pain and suffering. He gave me a check to deposit in your account in the amount of eighteen thousand dollars to pay for any future medical needs you might have," the banker added. He told Papa to sign the paper, freeing Mr. Norton from any further obligation. Papa signed the paper and used that money four years later to buy the rest of the 1200 acres that made up the family farm."

Dad stood up to stretch for a minute and then sat back down. "Your Uncle Fed was hired full time as a deputy sheriff a year later, promoted to county sheriff when Sheriff Dickson retired two years after that and then was elected to office twice. Fed was now a politician, courting the voters of Glynn County, speaking at political rallies and fundraisers, paying more attention to local, state and national politics. He never could quit thinking about that meeting at Jekyll Island…the secrecy of it all…plans to deceive the Congress and the people of the U.S.…to rig the presidential election…to underhandedly gain total control of the nation's banking system. In 1912 when Teddy Roosevelt entered the election as a third party candidate it split the vote just as they said it would, electing their man Woodrow Wilson. 'They did it…damned if they didn't do exactly what they said they would do,' Fed said to me."

Dad poured more iced tea and continued, "Fed talked with bankers and politicians at the state level as well as our District Congressman and one of our Senators, trying to understand the magnitude of Federal Reserve System which these powerful men had created at Jekyll Island and forced upon the American people. Fed couldn't keep quiet about what he perceived as a conspiracy by the powerful, rich bankers and corrupt politicians...delved into the subject often... with anyone he thought could lead him to some answers."

"One day our local state senator told Fed that he should stop this obsession of his right now. 'The powers that be will not let you continue with your accusations. They're gonna shut you up, Fed. It's causing too much controversy within the State of Georgia.' Of course Fed didn't stop... kept right on talking."

"I was with Fed in his office while he was opening the mail one morning. He pulled out a wanted poster with a letter from the Georgia Bureau of Investigation attached to it. Larry Carmichael was wanted for murder and bank robbery in Atlanta. The state police had a detail of troopers after him. He was on the run...last seen in Macon...believed to be headed to Savannah or Brunswick. The letter described him as a dangerous and desperate man. Two days later he killed your Uncle Fed, ambushed him as he left his office. I'm telling you this because I believe that Carmichael was sent to murder Fed. He didn't accidentally bump into Fed. It was a deliberate act of murder. Carmichael was killed in a shootout with state police the following day, after they received an anonymous tip of his location."

Dad paused and slowly said, "I've been thinking about this ever since President Kennedy was assassinated last November…four months after he abolished the Federal Reserve and began printing our own U.S. dollars. I believe that the same people killed Fed and President Kennedy. Isn't it interesting that the murderers of both men were themselves quickly killed before they could be questioned about their involvement in the killings? I wanted someone in the family to know… that's why I'm telling you."

One

Dad sold the farm in 1942, just a few months before I was born on March 7, 1943, the last of eight children...six girls and two boys... born to Chess Alexander Fleming and Geneva Hutcheson Fleming. He fought the depression and its low farm prices for as long as he could but in the end, like many "South Georgia sodbusters" he gave up the fight. He always said that if their first four born had been boys rather than all girls, as it turned out, he could have made our family farm pay. "Teenage girls weren't much help when you were tryin' to grow corn and cotton," he would say. Mom wanted to hang on a little longer, but she grudgingly gave in to Dad. They sold the 143 acres near Brunswick, Georgia and paid off all of their debts. With the little money that was left, they moved the whole family to the port city of Savannah, a very busy place with World War II going on.

Dad had already secured a job with an international roofing manufacturer, working on a machine that made felt roofing shingles. The hourly pay wasn't much, "But they have good benefits, including a pension," he would say. The job was hot and steamy but it was easy compared to the hard work he was accustomed to doing on the farm, and it was only an eight hour shift instead of a 12-14 hour workday. Dad excelled at it and within two years he was promoted to Machine Operator, supervising a crew of seven men on that machine. At 49, Dad could "outwork every man on the crew," according to his 46 year-old plant foreman and they were all in their twenties. They all called him, respectfully, "Uncle Chess." He had only an eighth grade education, but he could handle everything this job threw at him. He would work there until he retired, with his pension and gold pin.

There were just too many mouths to feed, so Mom went to work, also, in the summer of 1943. At 5'2", she was exactly what they were looking for at the Savannah Shipyard for a program that would train many small women to become welders. They could more easily fit into the cramped spaces on the merchant marine cargo ships that were brought in for repair, than their male co-workers. The pay was good and she loved the job…much easier than eight kids and a farm. She worked hard, became a very skilled welder and made herself valuable to the shipyard. In just a short period of time she had become their best at "overhead welding" and was often assigned special tasks when this difficult skill was required. Most of the welders were laid off in 1946 after the war ended, but Mom and a few others stayed on for another year to handle the few ships that came in for repair.

With Mom out of the house and all of my sisters and brothers in school, my sister, Beth, and I had to be looked after. Beth is two years older. There was a seven-year period, after our first six siblings were born, in which no children were born. Then quickly, Beth and I happened along. Dad would lovingly kid Mom, "If it hadn't been for that newly-scheduled midnight train coming through, Beth and Dan might not be here." She never failed to gasp when he said that. It was almost as if we had two families, the first six and then Beth and me. Mom tried a few nannies to keep us during the day and none of them seemed to be right. Then she hired Rebecca and everything changed for the better…changed my life.

Rebecca West was 25 years old with three children, two girls, three and five years old and Ben who was my age. She was a pretty lady, always neatly dressed, a bright and enchanting smile and a soft and kind voice that made you want to turn and listen when she spoke…never raising her voice. I learned to love Rebecca. Her husband, Johnnie, was still in Europe…a Master Sergeant in an all-black infantry unit. He had been wounded and sent to a hospital in England. After three months, he returned to his unit on the front lines. His Purple Heart Medal was sent to Rebecca and she talked about it to everyone. She was so proud of her hero. Her mother was a school teacher and she encouraged Rebecca to go to college. She went to Savannah State College at night and managed to complete two years before Ben was born. She was my "nanny" for nine years. After getting her girls off to school, Rebecca would arrive at our house each morning with Ben and feed us kids breakfast. She had a variety of jobs to do in the cooking, cleaning and laundry category each day...a list of things that mom specifically wanted done...and she always had dinner ready at 5 pm when mom got home from work.

The one thing I liked best about Rebecca was that she read story books to us each day for twenty minutes before she put us down for our naps. My favorite one was the story of "Johnnie Appleseed" with Rebecca singing the Johnnie Appleseed song at the end:

> "The Lord is good to me, and so I thank the Lord...for giving me the things I need...the sun and rain and the apple seed...the Lord is good to me."

What a beautiful voice she had...the lead singer in her church choir...made going to sleep easy. She also read to us from a Bible story book that had many color depictions of Bible scenes. I remember that at each Christmas she would try to explain to us the "real meaning of Christmas." She would eventually teach Ben and me to read at an early age.

Mom was a great seamstress. She made almost all of the girls' dresses and they were beautiful. Their girlfriends at school were envious. They were always trying to get Mom to make one for them. She had an old Singer sewing machine, the manual one with the wide foot pedal. Rebecca had used one in a Home Economics class in school, but was not skilled in its use. Mom spent a few late afternoons with her on that old Singer and before long Rebecca was turning out dresses for her girls and was doing some mending and alterations for Mom. While Rebecca was busy with chores and her sewing, she had less time to spend with us kids, and that was okay with Ben and me. There were plenty of kids our age in the neighborhood to play with, and Ben and I loved getting outside and mixing it up with the others. The neighborhood was one of government housing, single floor, ground level concrete block structures with four apartments in each unit. They backed up to each other to form a horseshoe.

Inside of the horseshoe was a grassy area of about 200 feet on each side, forming a square. Each parent could step out on their back porch and quickly view all that was going on in the play area. They were quick to step out when they heard a lot of screaming and yelling going on when we had a dispute of some kind that was leading to a fight. We kids all played in this area all day long... kids from three years to twelve years...sometimes in various groups and sometimes all together, depending on the games we played...kickball, stickball, baseball, football, cowboys and Indians, kick the can, hide and seek and racing each other. We had practically no adult supervision. The older kids taught the younger kids rules of the games and the mechanics of throwing, catching and hitting a ball or the skills of making your own bows and arrows.

But one thing no one had to teach Ben and me was how to run...fast. It came naturally, a blessing. We knew from the age of four that we had this gift of foot speed. The older kids saw it in us, too, and would become frustrated as we ran them down in a game of touch football...as we ran away from them when one of us had the ball. I was just a little faster than Ben, partly because I was taller. We would race each other every day as we grew up and I was always a little faster than him. Ben was okay with being second. He knew that no one else could run faster. We were getting close because we spent so much time together...becoming pals...inseparable. But that would end soon, after just nine years, through no fault of our own...and I hated it.

Now, I always knew that Ben was different...his skin was black. But that was okay...his momma's skin was black. And that's the way most of the kids in the neighborhood saw it, too. It wasn't a big deal. Oh, they might say something like, "Man, that little nigger can run," but they were just repeating something that they had heard...had no understanding of the word. But then, at age six, it was time to start elementary school. At first, it was hard for me to understand that I would be going to a school for white kids and that Ben would go to a school where only black kids would attend. Rebecca's explanation was, "That's just the way it is....it seems that nobody can do anything about it." That's pretty much what my parents said, too. Ben would come over after school every day and we would play ball with the other kids until Mom came home from work and Rebecca left for the day.

During the summer after completing the first and second grades, Ben would come with Rebecca every day, just like it was before we started elementary school. We would play together almost every day. Then, at nine years of age, our friendship would end when Mom and Dad announced that we would be building a new house in a community three miles away. We both cried on that cold day in January when my family packed the last of our belongings and moved to our new home in Garden City...thought we would never see each other again. What we viewed as the end of our friendship would turn out to be only a separation, however.

Growing up in the late forties and the entire decade of the fifties was an experience of togetherness, for family and community. Times were simpler and more innocent. People had time to sit out on their front porch after supper and greet neighbors as they walked by or as they worked in their yards across the street. It was a time when people looked out for each other and each others' kids…a time when you could let your kids ride their bikes to the community swimming pool and not be afraid that they would be harmed in any manner.

Mom quit her job at Hogan's Department store, working as the store's alterations person, when we moved to Garden City. She had worked there for five years after being laid off at the shipyard. By that time Rebecca was nearly as good as Mom was at sewing, so Mom recommended her for the job as her replacement. She got the job after a brief training and observation period and much deliberation. There were a few managers who objected to hiring a black woman for this job. Mom was proud of Rebecca…the grace with which she handled her critics…the quiet manner of tolerance she exhibited with a "particular" kind of customer now and then. Mom spent three weeks breaking Rebecca in for the job and never once did she have reason to regret recommending her. Rebecca worked in that job for four years, obviously doing a good job, and quit when she finally graduated from college and became a teacher.

Two

Garden City was a unique little incorporated town of three hundred homes. In 1952 when we moved there, the roads were not paved. The city's road scraper came by periodically, especially after it rained, and smoothed out the ruts in the roads. The roads were finally paved in 1957. The town had its own water supply, as was evidenced by the huge water tower that could be seen from all around. The siren calling for the volunteer firemen to report was mounted on top of the water tower. We had a police department consisting of the chief and one or two deputies. Almost everyone went to church each Sunday to one of the four churches in Garden City - Baptist, Methodist, Presbyterian and Lutheran. There were a few Catholics, but they had to drive three miles to the nearest Catholic Church.

Most of the people who lived in Garden City were hourly paid workers employed in the many factories along the Savannah River. No one had a whole lot of money so much of the work done to improve the community was done by volunteers. Volunteers built ball fields, Boy Scout houses and campsite areas, picnic areas and a community center where all kinds of events were held…from city elections to wedding receptions…dances to birthday parties. It was here, in the fifties, that I would grow up to adulthood. It's where I would learn values from my family, Sunday school teachers, coaches, scout leaders, preachers and church leaders that would shape my life into the man that I would become.

Life was uncomplicated in "Fifties Garden City." In the early fifties much of family entertainment was centered around the radio. Savannah didn't get a local TV station until 1954. We would gather around the radio with Mom and Dad after dinner and listen to programs like "Lum and Abner," "Jack Benny," "Gunsmoke," "The Grand Ole Opry," and a news commentator, Gabriel Heater, the Rush Limbaugh of their day. Mom and Dad didn't like to miss Gabriel Heater. I had afternoon favorites like "Sergeant Preston of the Yukon," "The Lone Ranger," "Roy Rogers," and "Gene Autry." My friends and I would stop whatever game we were playing at five o'clock and go to the nearest house and listen to our radio programs.

At first I missed Ben very much. I made friends quickly, however…lots of boys my age in the new neighborhood….plenty of activities and fun. There were Cub Scouts and camping. We camped out a lot in our pup tents, a big adventure sleeping out in the woods and preparing breakfast next morning over an open fire. Almost every day we played baseball or football on vacant lots near our homes or basketball at the community center, depending on the season. There was no adult supervision, only pickup games. Usually teams were centered on geographical locations, our east side taking on The Rommel Avenue west side, for example. We took it seriously and the competition was fierce at times…loved to compete and win. There were no trophies to be given out to the victors, only the satisfaction of winning…that was enough.

We didn't have organized little leagues until 1955, when I was twelve years old. At nine, ten and eleven years of age I was beginning to excel in sports. I was still faster than the others and that gave me an edge. I was discovering that I had a strong throwing arm, too. I was quarterback on the football team, pitcher and shortstop on the baseball team and point guard on the basketball team. "Playing ball" became my life. It was all I wanted to do. As the season changed from one sport to another I would put one ball up and take out another. It was hard to give up Boy Scouts because I loved it, too, but there just wasn't time for it.

It wasn't all fun and games, though. I had chores to do at home and Mom and Dad encouraged us to earn money when we had the opportunity. At ten and eleven years I earned two dollars each week by delivering flyers to homes in Garden City for Tomlinson's Supermarket. Mr. Tomlinson would print up his weekly price leaders for meats and groceries on an 8 x 11 sheet of colored paper. Each Wednesday after school I would walk to his store and pick up the flyers packed in a canvas bag with a shoulder strap, and walk the streets, stuffing one flyer in each mailbox.

At twelve years of age I got the cream job of the neighborhood. Only two guys got this job. A friend, who was two years older, quit for a higher paying job and recommended me. I would be working for the Mayor of Garden City, Mr. Arthur Rowell, who was involved in several enterprises. Mr. Rowell had a contract to deliver the Savannah Morning News to each subscriber in Garden City. Pete Hodges was the other guy, a good friend who lived around the corner from me, just five houses away. Our job was to collect payment from subscribers to the newspaper each Wednesday after school. Mr. Rowell would drive his station wagon down each street with Pete and me in the back seat. I would do one side of the street and Pete would take the other. The rate for each subscriber was $1.80 for a month. We would knock on the door and yell, "collect for the Morning News." They would almost always come to the door with two one-dollar bills and we would always have two silver dimes change for them. We would bring the two dollars back to the car and Mr. Rowell would enter payment in his ledger.

Mr. Rowell surely had his customers organized. Because he drove the same route each week, customers knew just about what time we would get there, so they were expecting us. Pete and I were both quick and we hustled, so we got through faster...Mr. Rowell liked that. I liked getting paid three dollars per week, a lot of money for a twelve year-old boy. I gave Mom two dollars each week and saved the rest for things I needed like a baseball glove and basketball shoes...and going to the movies.

Once or twice each month Pete, Butch Parks or Jimmy Crosby and I would walk to the city bus stop and for a dime ride to downtown Savannah and back. There we would watch movies all day. My favorites were the westerns...Roy Rogers, Gene Autry, Lash LaRue and Rocky Lane. Plus serial movies, the kind that ended each week with the hero in a predicament that he surely couldn't escape from....so you just had to come back next Saturday to see how Superman or Batman got out of it. A double feature at the State Theater was a dime, and then another two at the Bijou was fifteen cents...four full length movies for only a quarter. The theaters didn't just show movies.

They always had some kind of special guest or entertainment going on during intermission. It was exciting to see heroes such as Lash LaRue in person, giving an exhibition with his bull whip, after seeing him in the movies. Intermission at the Bijou would always include an MC who would lead us in sing-a-longs such as "Cruising Down the River," and he would call out the numbers of winning tickets for prize drawings. In between the two theaters, The State and The Bijou, we could go to the Krystal in the next block and get two burgers, fries and a coke for forty cents. Four movies, lunch, and a bus ride to town for only seventy-five cents...what a bargain.

At one of the movie intermissions our entertainment was two world yoyo champions putting on a display of their skills. Seeing that, I just had to have a new "Filipino Twirler." It was a challenge that I loved and everywhere I went I had my yoyo in my pocket. I practiced all of the time and two years later won the tournament held at the Bijou. The prize was a precision-balanced Filipino Twirler made of wood. I was so proud of it because I could never justify paying for one. I wore that one out eventually...too many loop-de-loops, shooting stars, rock the cradles, round the worlds and spank the babies.

I came across a similar one years later that was of the same quality and price. I bought it happily and renewed my interest. I still have it today, put away in a safe place to protect it from those who might not appreciate its worth. I get it out occasionally to impress grandchildren, neighbors and guests, but mostly it's for me....for fun. I wish kids today could embrace the challenge of mastering the yoyo and experience that joy of accomplishment that I felt...the pure fun of it...knowing that for one day you were the best at it. I haven't seen an electronic game that can do that.

Another game we played was the game of "marbles." Shooting a marble was a difficult skill to learn, and the only way you could learn it was from the others boys in the neighborhood. I had watched the older boys play and was amazed at the skill some of them displayed when shooting a marble with their thumb, at how accurate they could be. I liked the prestige that went with being a winning marble player. The best players from our area would take on the best players from other parts of the neighborhood from time to time in order to establish a champion. I liked the special attention given to the big winners and especially the one who became the champion...knew that this was what I wanted to be. I began practicing, watching, learning, and over time I got better and better.

To play the game, a circle about three feet in diameter was drawn on a smoothly prepared piece of ground. Each player, usually three or four boys, would put two or three of their marbles into the center of the ring. The object was to shoot a marble from outside the ring and knock as many marbles out of the ring as you could. Your shooter must stay inside of the ring in order for you to keep the marbles that you knocked out of the ring. If your shooter went out of the ring, you lost your turn and the marbles you knocked out had to be put back into the center of the ring. The winner was the one with the most marbles. Good marble players could win a lot of marbles, and I did. I started playing the game when I was five years old. At first I played only "funsies" with the older guys while they were teaching me to play…couldn't afford to lose too many marbles. I improved rapidly, though, and soon was playing "keeps" with the other guys. We were allowed to play marbles at school during recess periods. That's where I won a lot of marbles. I would take my favorite shooter and six marbles with me to school each day. Most days I would come home with twenty-five to forty marbles. By the time I was eleven years old I had over a thousand marbles in a wooden cheese keg, marbles that I had won.

I never questioned why we didn't have organized Little League baseball in Garden City. I knew that there were three other areas in Savannah where Little Leagues had been around for several years. They had a playoff each year to decide a City Champion. I had seen them play in their colorful uniforms and I was envious, especially since I thought we could beat them. I wasn't envious for long, though. Next summer, 1955, we had our little league on the west side of Savannah. Mr. Austin Stafford and Mr. Joseph Simpson saw the desire in us kids and organized the sponsors and the coaches to support our four-team league. Each team had a sponsor that provided the uniforms, enough bats and balls for the season and catchers equipment. My team was sponsored by Slotin and Company, a wholesale dry goods company. It was owned by Harry Slotin who was a Korean War hero. We had white uniforms with green stripes, green hats, green socks, green numbers and "Slotin" printed in green across the front. I was so proud of those uniforms. Mr. Simpson was our coach and he really taught us a lot about the game that summer.

I was our team's number one pitcher…we had three. Games were six innings long and league rules allowed you to pitch only six innings per week. When I wasn't eligible to pitch, I played shortstop which I enjoyed more. We won our League championship and would be going to the Savannah City Series against the winners of the other three leagues.

The championship series would be a single game elimination, lose and you're out. The first two games of the championship series were on a Monday afternoon at 5 pm. The winners would play each other for the championship on Wednesday at 5 pm. I pitched the first game and we won four to one over the American League Champions. The National League champions won the other game so we would meet them Wednesday at 5 pm for the Savannah Championship. This was great except for one little problem...Pete Hodges, our first baseman, and I had to work from 3 to 7 pm each Wednesday for Mr. Rowell, collecting for the Morning News. Mr. Rowell would not let us off to play the game...didn't matter to him that it was for the city championship. Mr. Simpson talked to him but he wouldn't budge from his decision. His customers depended upon him showing up at the same time each week to collect payment and he wasn't about to experience the confusion that it would cause if we didn't show up this week. Pete and I were just sick. Mom and Dad agreed with Mr. Rowell. "You've made a commitment to a job and you need to stick to it," Dad said. Pete's parents said the same thing so we thought it must be the right thing to do.

Pete and I were happy that Mr. Rowell picked us up a few minutes early the day of the game. We didn't think that it was possible to complete our work in time to make the game, but we had to try. We would literally sprint from the car to the front porch of each house, collect the money quickly and sprint back to the car. After a few minutes of this Mr. Rowell saw what was going on. He didn't say anything to acknowledge our efforts, but he began writing faster as he entered each payment into the ledger book. It was clear that we were moving along a lot faster on the route than normal, but after nearly two hours it was also clear that we would not finish in time to play the game. Mr. Rowell could see the anguish and disappointment on our faces as time began to slip away from us. And a few minutes later he couldn't help but notice the tears and the quiver and crack in our voices as we spoke. Finally he said, "Okay boys, at the next house each of you ask to use the phone. Call your homes and ask your parents to meet us at the ball field with your uniforms, and I'll take you to the field." We knew we couldn't hug the Mayor of Garden City, but we surely felt like it.

Pete and I just knew that we would be late for the game but when we arrived the Mayor of Savannah and other dignitaries were still speaking, delaying the game for twenty minutes. We quickly changed into our uniforms and took the field with our team, Pete at first base and I at shortstop. Both teams' No. 1 and No.2 pitchers had used up all of their eligible innings, so both No. 3 pitchers were on the mound. Walter Saucier was our pitcher. He had pitched only a few innings during the season, but he was ready for the challenge. Mr. Simpson told us that the team who wins this game will be the one who scores the most runs, so today we had to hit the ball well and run the bases with no mistakes. Walter pitched the whole game and he did all that our coach asked of him. He didn't walk many batters and trusted us in the field to get them out when we had the opportunity. They scored a lot of runs, nine of them. We scored twelve runs, however, and became City Champions in just our first year in organized baseball. We were so happy…and proud. Pete and I accounted for six of our fifteen hits and five runs batted in…and that made Mr. Rowell proud. Even though he kept his cigar in his mouth during the whole game, we could tell that he was smiling. He knew that he had done a good thing.

We received two trophies that year, one for winning our league championship and one for being City Champs. We were disappointed to learn that our team would not be going to state and regional playoffs in order to advance to the Little League World Series held in Williamsport, Pennsylvania. It seems that the prospect of playing against black kids could not be allowed by local officials. It was the position of many southern cities in 1955. Never mind the world! We were city champs and that's all that mattered to us at the time.

Seventh grade was the last year of elementary school, so we were the "big kids." Our teacher was Mrs. McGowan, not to be confused with a teacher of the same name who taught fifth grade. I loved Mrs. McGowan. She had a special way to communicate the lessons of math, English, history and science…to inspire you to learn. One very special thing she did, however, was to teach us the Bible from beginning to end. Each morning, for twenty minutes, she would read to us from a special edition of the Bible, translated in language that was easily understood by twelve year olds. It was the highlight of my day. Mrs. McGowan made the Bible come alive for us, in a way that didn't happen in our Sunday school classes at church, where we read from the King James Version of the Bible. What I learned that year gave me a basic knowledge of Bible history that would help me the rest of my life as I studied God's word. What a gift she was to our class. She probably didn't have a clue that at some time in the future she would be stopped from reading her Bible to her students.

Junior high school was two years of double session classes, with our school sharing the facilities of another school in downtown Savannah. We had classes from 7 am until noon and the other school had the building from noon until 5 pm. In two years the county would build us a new school in Garden City, Robert W. Groves High School, which would include grades eight through twelfth. But until then it would mean catching the school bus at six o'clock each morning with five fifty-minute classes each day.

It was here that I met my favorite teacher ever, Mrs. Beulah Harper. I was in her eighth and ninth grade English classes and her first year Latin class in the ninth grade. She was a rare combination of Southern charm and class. Mrs. Harper was always pleasant...humorous. Behind that wonderful smile, however, she was tough. She pushed us hard those two years, expecting a lot out of us…and she got it. She motivated us to do things that we never thought we could do. I was deathly afraid to stand before the class to give an oral report. She informed us that we would do four during the year of ninth grade English. Doing my first oral report, I was mortified… didn't crack a smile….me, the class clown…it was awful. After such a failure, I told Mrs. Harper that I just couldn't do that again and asked if I could do some extra work to make up for the remaining three oral reports. She took me aside and said, "Dan, you're the quarterback on our football team, a confident leader. I have seen you play and I know you can do this. Four years ago a similar thing happened to one of my students when he spoke in front of the class for the first time, and he was the captain of the basketball team. I told him the same thing that I'm telling you now, that it will be easier the second time and even easier the third. On your fourth report you'll be your usual, jovial self while you speak to us. By the way, that student is a senior now and he is Student Council President, Rex Glisson. Now he comfortably speaks before different groups all of the time." She was so right. With her encouragement it did get easier for me that year to stand before the class and give an oral presentation. She was somewhat prophetic, too, because I, too, would become Student Council President my senior year, the third president of our new school's student body.

I played Junior League baseball for ages thirteen through fifteen during the three summers after Little League. The team was sponsored by the Savannah Sugar Refinery and our coach was Gene "Buzz" Weston. Mr. Weston once pitched for the St. Louis Browns in the 1930's. His son, Bubba, played second base for us and he showed us old newspaper clippings which told of Mr. Weston striking out Babe Ruth and Lou Gehrig and other accomplishments. We had a lot of respect for him and his knowledge of the game. He taught us a lot about hitting and fielding in those three years. Our Junior League infield of Leon Richardson at catcher, Pete Hodges at first base, Bubba Weston at second base, Danny Stevens at shortstop and me at third base would play on the starting team for Groves High School for four years, starting as freshmen. Each of us would go on to play baseball in college or professionally.

Three

In the fall of 1959 I began my sophomore year in our brand new high school building in Garden City. It was so exciting....new facilities... lots of new teachers...a whole new attitude and school spirit. My sister, Beth, a majorette, would be in the first graduating class. I played first team defensive back on our football team and third team quarterback. I was second team point guard on the basketball team, but I got to play quite a bit. My baseball coach told me that he wanted more speed in the outfield so he moved me from third base to center field. I had a good year hitting and led the region in stolen bases.

I had my best day of the year when we played a doubleheader with cross town rival Benedictine, the private Catholic school. Their star was Ken Harrelson, a senior, who went on to play for the Athletics, Yankees and White Sox where he became a radio announcer and later GM of the team. Scouts for the Phillies and the Pirates were at the game to see Ken. We won the first game. It was tied when I came to bat in the sixth inning with two runners on base. I nailed a knee high fastball and hit a low line drive straight at the center fielder. He charged in for the ball only to see it rising over his head. Both runs scored and I ended up with a triple. In their last at bat, Benedictine had runners on first and second with two outs. A low line drive was hit to me and I charged it, thinking that I could catch it on the fly. It was a sinking line drive, though, and at the last second I knew it would hit the ground just in front of me. Still on a dead run, I slid to my knees with my glove in front of me to block the ball, to keep it from getting by me and allowing both runs to score. Luckily I trapped the ball cleanly, bounced up from my knees, still on the run, and with the help of my forward momentum was able to throw a one hop strike to home plate to nail the runner and end the game. We lost the second game to a pair of Ken Harrelson home runs.

After the game both scouts were asking our coach about Bubba, Danny, Leon and me. They said that I made one of the best plays that they had seen from center field...the play that ended the first game. Coach told the scouts that we were only sophomores and they both said that they would be back in two years. It was fun playing baseball at that level at such a young age.

That day I began to believe that I had a shot at playing professional baseball. When Ken Harrelson signed with the Kansas City Royals, I was even more encouraged….baseball was to be my future. I had dreams of a playing and coaching career that would last a lifetime. I had a good baseball season, batting .328 and leading the region in stolen bases.

I also ran the hundred yard dash for our track team that spring, my first effort at this sport. I didn't get to practice much because it conflicted with baseball practice and games. I would just show up at meets when I could. The coaches were okay with this arrangement. I won a 3-team meet with a time of 10.6 seconds, a good effort for me. I looked at the track meet results next morning in the Savannah Morning News and noticed that Ben West had won the 100-yard dash in a 3-team meet of black schools with a time of 10.3 seconds. I thought about calling him, but it seemed so complicated…and it had been so long. What would I say? Maybe he will see our results and call me. What mattered…we were still the fastest.

During the summers after my sophomore and junior years I worked as a brick mason helper. The masonry company was owned by Dave Stewart's dad and brothers and he got me the job. Dave was just graduated from Groves High School and though he was two years ahead of me in school we became good friends. It was very hard work in the hot South Georgia sun, carrying wheel barrow loads of bricks and concrete blocks to the masons, mixing mortar and carrying it in wheel barrows to the masons, building and tearing down steel scaffolds and cleaning up at the end of a 7 am-3 pm workday. I built a lot of character that first summer. They paid me $1.25 per hour... thought I was rich. I put over six hundred dollars in my college savings account that summer.

My junior year at Robert W. Groves High School was life changing for me. Our head football coach, Jim Reynolds, announced that he would be leaving us for a new job as principal of our cross town rival, Jenkins High School. We all knew that he had been working on his Masters Degree, but we didn't know that it would take him away from us for a better job. I can see why he would get the promotion....he was a man of the highest character. We were disappointed, but we liked our new head coach right away. It was Bubba Atwood's first head coaching job. He came with a lot of enthusiasm and we caught it. He devised a whole new offensive scheme and it seemed to fit me to a "T". I would play first team left halfback and backup quarterback. On defense I would play left cornerback. We had a good preseason practice with a lot of plays designed to take advantage of my speed...wide pitchouts to get me outside of the end...swing passes in the flat...and a few long passes downfield. I was in the best physical condition ever...muscles honed for strength and perseverance by the hard work I did on those 8 to 10 hour work days during the summer, while playing baseball games at night. My hopes were the highest ever as I began my junior year at Groves High School. I was so excited to play our first game of the year against rival Savannah High School on September 18, 1959, not knowing that it would turn out terribly for me and our team.

On our second possession of the ball, I was tackled after a short gain and there was a big pileup....with me on the bottom, facedown. My right hand was holding the football against my side and my left arm was outstretched....hand flat on the ground. During the unpiling procedure, one of the several big linemen on top of me jumped up in the middle of the pile and stepped on my left hand with his spikes. The pain was excruciating. My hand went numb immediately, bleeding from three places where the different spikes punctured my hand. Our team doctor, Dr. Nash, looked at it on the sidelines. He cleaned and dressed it and said that I should sit out a few plays. Well, I wasn't about to sit on the bench after working so hard to make the first team, so I was back in there the next time we had the ball, even though my hand was beginning to swell.

We were deep in our own territory and a pitchout to me was called. Being the left halfback and moving out to my left meant that my left hand would be primarily responsible for catching the ball. It was a perfect pitch, but when it touched my left hand I felt nothing. When I closed my right hand over the ball it was already rolling away from my left hand, falling to the ground. Savannah High recovered the fumble and I felt awful when they scored a few plays later, their only score of the game. We scored later in the game but missed the extra point, losing the game 7 to 6. In my mind I had lost the game for us…felt sick…didn't go out with my friends after the game. I didn't sleep at all that night and it wasn't because of the pain I felt in my hand. I relived that fumbled pitchout over and over in my mind all night long.

The game was Friday night and Dr. Nash didn't normally work on Saturday, but he said that he wanted me to meet him at the hospital in the morning for X-Rays. Saturday morning my hand was so swollen that it was perfectly round. It looked more like a ham hock hanging on the end of my arm instead of a hand. The X-Rays showed that the knuckle of my left ring finger was crushed and that there were multiple fractures of my corresponding fourth left metacarpal, extending up into my hand, almost to my wrist. Dr. Nash set my hand and positioned my shattered knuckle in a hard cast that covered my hand and beyond my wrist. I had to keep it in a sling for four weeks. He told me that my football season was over. That was tough to take. Something that was so important to me was taken away in just a matter of hours. What I didn't know at the time was that things would get worse. I continued to practice with the team, avoiding any contact in scrimmages and just trying to stay in condition. In the back of my mind I still thought that I would heal in time to play our last two games.

As the football season progressed I began to see a star running back mature to greatness. Ben West was his name, and he played for the Thompkins High Wolverines. It was common on any given night to read about Ben making touchdown runs of forty to eighty yards. It was interesting that we were about the same size, five feet eight inches tall and 160 pounds. I really wanted to see him play, so one Saturday night in November three of my team mates and I went to watch one of his games. We were the only white people at the game. Ben's moves were smooth and lightning quick. On the third play from scrimmage he ran 68 yards for a score, ran a punt back 82 yards for a touchdown and caught a swing pass in the flat and turned up field 56 yards for another score. I was happy for him...something special, Ben was. He was as good as sportswriters were saying, definitely college material. I went away from that game depressed. Ben was in his glory and I couldn't even get into a game. Life is not fair. After the game I told the guys the story of Ben and me growing up together...of his mother being my nanny...that Ben and I were friends. They didn't believe me, thought I was making it up.

On November 12, Dr. Nash removed my cast and took X-Rays. He wasn't happy with the outcome and neither was I. My knuckle was locked into position with my ring finger pointed up as I looked at the palm of my hand. This just wouldn't do. I could never catch a baseball, a forward pass in a football game or a cross court pass in a basketball game. Plus, it looked as if I was giving the finger to someone when I held my hand a certain way. That could get me into a lot of trouble. It had to be fixed. Mom and Dad agreed to a procedure that would require breaking the knuckle and the metacarpal again, then inserting a three inch steel pin through the middle of the knuckle and the broken metacarpal. It would be held in place and with another hard plaster cast to stabilize it for eight to ten weeks. I was crushed. That meant that I would miss the remaining two football games and most of the basketball season, if not all of it.

Coach John McGinty, our basketball coach, allowed me to practice with the team right from the beginning of the season, even though I was ineligible to play in games because of the hard cast on my hand. I stayed in good condition and after a couple of weeks of practice, with foam rubber taped over my cast to prevent me from hurting my teammates, it was clear that I would play a lot once I became eligible. The cast came off January 21, 1960...and it was somewhat of a success. My left ring finger knuckle joint was no longer locked in a fixed positioned. It would straighten out when I laid it flat on a table, but it was not completely flexible as it was before the injury. It would not close completely into a fist along with the other fingers of my left hand. I didn't start any of the remaining basketball games, but I came off the bench early each game and played a lot. Our team had a winning season, but lost out in the regional tournament. My left hand stayed sore all of the time, but it was something I had to work through.

Baseball practice began in March. Nearly every starter was back from the previous year. Most of us were juniors, already with two years of experience, so we were favored to be City Champions. I would return to third base from my center field position of last year. My spring was busy. On top of baseball I still ran the 100-yard dash on the track team when track meets didn't conflict with my baseball games. We were city champs again and I made the All City team at third base and led the region in stolen bases for the second time.

I won only one meet with a time of 10.6 seconds. I noticed in the newspaper that Ben won, again, for Thompkins High, in a meet against other black schools, with a time 10.2. There must have been a strong wind at his back. I bet I can still beat him in a straight up foot race...always did...think I'll give him a call.

As it turned out I didn't need to call him. Next week after baseball practice, I was sitting on one of the concrete benches in front of the school, near Wheat Hill Road which ran by our school. I was just relaxing a bit before I started my walk home...lived only four blocks from school. I watched as a black guy turned off of the main highway onto Wheat Hill Road, walking toward me. I thought little of this because I had observed this scene before. There were lots of black families living on Wheat Hill Road...beyond our school... across the railroad tracks. He walked on the edge of the road, on the opposite side of where I was sitting. But this time it was different. I couldn't take my eyes off of him as he walked toward me. As he got closer, he must have sensed my staring...began to look back at me, curiously staring, too. When he drew even with me, just a few feet separating us, he stopped and turned to face me. His track shoes with the laces tied together were draped over his shoulder...a big wide grin on his face...I knew...he knew.

"Ben?" I asked.

"Dan?" was his answer.

The emotion was overwhelming. I spoke with a quiver in my voice that I had never heard...just sat there on the bench...looking up...him standing in front of me now...looking down. "Sit down, let's talk," I said.

"Don't think that's a good idea. Lots of people are still coming out of your school...might create a buzz," he whispered. I didn't care what someone might think. I just wanted to talk to my friend, something I hadn't done in eight years. We didn't shake hands or hug. We just looked at each other and talked for over an hour. Ben asked where I lived...about Mom, Dad and Beth. I gave him a brief account of the past eight years. He wanted to know about my hand...read about the injury in the newspaper. I quizzed him about Rebecca... now teaching third grade. One of his sisters was a freshman in college and the oldest was in her senior year. Ben's dad retired from the Army in 1959 as a Sergeant Major with twenty years service, and was now working at the National Paper mill, the world's largest paper mill, employing over five thousand people. He had fought in two of our country's wars and was wounded in both. He received another Purple Heart Medal during the Korean War and was one of that war's most decorated soldiers. Ben was so happy to have him home again, fulltime. His face would light up as he told of how his dad got him interested in playing football three years ago. He had played football in college, a running back, and knew a lot about the game. They moved out of the housing project four years ago and bought a house on Wheat Hill Road, just across the railroad tracks, four blocks from Groves High School and only a half a mile from my house. Ben and I lived less than half a mile from each other for four years and didn't know it. But, you see, only blacks lived on Wheat Hill Road beyond the railroad tracks, so we never went down there. How <u>could</u> we know? It was dark when we decided to break it up and go home.

"See ya," he said. I nodded with a smile and we both knew that we would see each other a lot more…that our friendship never ended…just took a hiatus.

I couldn't wait to get home that night and tell Mom. She had heard that Rebecca had become a school teacher like her mother from the women at Hogan's Store, but that was all. Mom was eager for me to fill her in on everything…was astonished that she lived so close to us. Mom could tell by my excitement that it wasn't just a one-time meeting…that Ben and I would get together again. I saw that worried look on her face.

"Better be careful, son. You know how some people are. They can make a lot of trouble for you...you and Ben," she warned.

As I entered school the next day I began to understand what she was saying…strange sideways looks…overt whispering for me to see… could they be talking about Ben and me….paid no attention to it. After baseball practice that afternoon, I walked down Wheat Hill Road, across the railroad tracks, to Ben's house. It was the second house on the right…steel chain length fence around it…new coat of white paint with black shutters next to the windows…covered porch all of the way across the front of the house…porch swing and rocking chairs…three steps leading up to the porch…lots of flowers, planted in beds out front, in flower pots and hanging baskets. I didn't need directions. I knew I was at Rebecca's house, and there she was, coming out of the door as I made it to the top step.

With that sweet Rebecca smile that I never put out of my memory she looked at me and said, "Come here, boy, and give me a hug!" I did.... could not control the tears. She didn't look like she aged at all, trim and smartly dressed as always. Her hair was shoulder length, pulled back and tied at her neck with her trademark pink ribbon, just as I remembered her. We went into the house and talked for a few minutes. Ben and his dad were at a track meet and would be home soon. He had told his mom that I might drop by today. She wanted to know all about Mom. I filled her in as much as I could before Ben came bounding in with John. This was the first time I had met Ben's dad. He was about Ben's size...a few pounds heavier...looked like he was in playing shape to me, though.

"I am pleased to meet you Mr. West. Ben has told me a lot about you," I said, as I reached to shake his hand.

"Just call me John," he said, as his hand firmly gripped mine. John was different than I had expected of a man who had a lot of military authority while he served in the Army. Being a battalion Sergeant Major, the top enlisted man who commanded over 1200 troops, he was accustomed to getting his way as he barked out orders. He was soft spoken, though, and he seemed to weigh his words carefully as he spoke to me...to us. He seemed genuinely interested in what I had to say as I talked with them. And I could tell that he honored and respected Rebecca by the way he spoke to her. Rebecca invited me to stay for dinner. I called Mom to see if it was okay. She said no at first, but when I told her that we were having "Rebecca's fried chicken" with mashed potatoes and gravy she gave in, knowing that it always was my favorite meal. We kept talking as we ate our meal…embarrassed myself by eating so much. I asked if I could help with the dishes, but Rebecca would not have it. She shooed Ben and me out to the front porch. We talked for another hour or so…about growing up as innocent little kids who would never understand why we had to live apart simply because of the color of our skin…about what is going on right now in our lives…about the future, college mostly. Ben was surprised that I went to one of his football games to watch him play. He told me that Florida A & M University is interested in offering him a football scholarship. I told him to take it. Who wouldn't want to play for coach Jake Gaither.

Just last week Ben was elected President of the Student Council of Thompkins High School for his senior year. What an honor on top of all of his football and track achievements. We swapped telephone numbers and agreed to call each other. My family was on a two-party line back in those days with our neighbors, Phil and Nancy Wilson. My sisters called her "Nosy Nancy" because she was always picking up the phone to listen in on their conversations, especially if they were talking to a boyfriend. I warned him to be careful of what he said during our phone conversations. He understood.

It was the first of May and a number of significant events were about to take place at Groves High School, apart from the fact that our baseball team was fighting again for the city championship. Our school began its three-week campaign to elect Student Council officers for the coming year. Candidates for each position were nominated from the various clubs…Key Club, Beta Club, Science Club, etc. The nominations were in and there was a lot of disagreement and downright dissatisfaction with those nominated for president. Many friends said that they just wouldn't bother voting. To that I simply said, "If you don't' vote, don't gripe."

That's when a few friends said, "Why don't you run for president?" That took me by surprise… didn't know how to answer except to say no. They persisted and the more I thought about it I said, "Why not?"….it could be fun….and I had a few ideas that I thought would help build traditions that would improve school spirit for our newly established school, just two years old.

The only problem was that you had to be nominated by one of the clubs, and those nominations had all been done. My only chance was to be a "write-in" candidate, and that's what I did.

I made sure that there was a place on the ballot for a write in candidate, so I had a chance….a slim one. It was much easier to just check off one of the names listed on the ballot than to remember my name and then go to the effort to write it in.

After getting the required number of signatures on a petition, I was accepted as an official write in candidate for president of the student council. I missed the first week and that left only one week of campaigning. I borrowed an idea from Ben that he used in his campaign to get elected President at his school. He had a red wagon that he fixed up like an old west covered wagon, using bamboo hoops and some canvas. I borrowed his wagon and constructed the canvas top. Painted on one side of the canvas was "Fleming for President…Just Write On The Ballot." On the other side was painted "President or Bust…Dan Fleming." Inside the wagon I had a surprise goodie each day to hand out to voters… Tootsie Rolls, chewing gum, suckers, etc. As I pulled the wagon through the halls between class periods a crowd would always follow me asking for the treat for the day. As I passed out the treats, I told them to remember that they must write my name on the ballot. Though I was a week behind the other candidates in starting my campaign, I could tell that I was gaining momentum. On the day of the election each candidate for president was required to give a campaign speech to the whole student body over the school's PA system.

Since my campaign slogan was "If you don't vote, don't gripe," I continued with that idea. My speech was not about a list of accomplishments or a list of things that I would like to see done to improve our school. It was short and to the point. I began by reminding everyone that there was a big difference between the other candidates and me....my name had to be written in the allotted space on the ballot if you are voting for me. Then I added:

> "But the most important thing about this election is not that you vote for me....or any other person who will speak to you today. What matters most is that you vote. The right to vote for our preferred way of life is the greatest freedom that we have as Americans. Those running for office might not be perfect in all things, but we have a duty to choose the best one, in our opinion, and vote for that person to lead us. And the habit of voting needs to start now, not when we are of legal age to vote in governmental elections. In our Student Council election last year only 54% of our student body went to the trouble to vote. I hope that we can do better than that in this election. It's not about who wins....it's that we all have a "say" in the outcome.... then we all win. Let's all vote...100% of us....it can be done....but only if you vote."

Voting was to take place immediately after our speeches were made and counted during second period. During third period it was announced over the PA system that I had won. I was the incoming Student Council President.

After my last class that day I went by Mrs. Sylvia Fauerstein's classroom. She taught our course in Civics, a study of government and politics. I wanted to thank her because my friends had been telling me all day long how she had bragged about my speech…of how she jumped up out of her chair and interrupted my speech over the speaker in her room...saying, "Listen to him, that's what I want you all to understand." I enjoyed my brief conversation with her… never talked to her before…just knew who she was. As I turned to go to baseball practice she said, "I expect you to be in my Civics class next year." I told her that I would for certain. What a wonderful person she proved to be…caring, dedicated, knowledgeable, fun…a wonderful teacher. She would greatly affect the rest of my life.

Our baseball team won the city championship but lost out in the regional playoff again. I was ordered by our Principal, Mr. Donald Gray, to take senior English during summer school. Having one less subject to worry about would free up more time to handle the business of being Student Council President during my senior year. It was a lot of studying to do, cramming a whole school year into ten weeks during the summer.

I still had time to work as a brick mason's helper with the Stewarts that summer and play baseball in the Savannah River League on Tuesday night, Thursday night and on Saturdays. The SRL was formed many years ago as an industrial league, where local factories sponsored teams for employees. It became very competitive and some factories hired former professional players to fill certain positions. I played for the Henderson Sporting Goods team. We were made up of mostly college and former college players. I was the youngest at seventeen. The oldest was John Dotson at 42. He bounced around the minor leagues for fifteen years before giving up. He couldn't run well, but he could still hit a baseball. I jokingly told him, "John, I believe you will still be able to hit a 90-mile fastball when they have to roll you up to the plate in a wheelchair." I batted .355 and made the all-star team at center field and led the league in stolen bases. I believed that I was running faster than ever. It was a very busy summer, taking senior English at summer school, playing baseball and working as a brick mason helper. I managed to add an additional 600 dollars to my college fund.

My injured hand healed over the summer and was strengthened by the hard physical labor that I was doing each day. Against my parent's wishes and Dr. Nash's advice, I decided that I would play football my senior year. I was two weeks late to fall practice because I had made a commitment to work and because baseball season was still going on. I believed that I could catch up, however, and worked extra hard to do so before our first game in two weeks. I knew right away that I could help the team, running the ball and pass receiving. I was in the best shape possible and faster than ever.

As I was coming out of locker room one day after football practice, I saw Ben walking down Wheat Hill Road to his home. He was just coming home from pre-season practice, too. I waved for him to come over. Coach Bob Olsen, our line coach, was the last one out of the locker room, locking up. He saw us and walked over. I introduced him to Ben. He said that he had been to three of his games just to watch him play.

"You have some kind of speed, Ben...and moves, too....hope you go on to play in college," Coach Olsen said.

"Hey Coach, Ben and I have raced hundreds of times as kids. I won them all," I kidded.

"But we were only nine years old!" Ben interjected.

I told him that I still could beat him in a one-on-one footrace, straight up. Coach Olsen said, "Dan, I've seen you run and I've seen Ben run. It would be close but I don't think you will win."

Then I said, "Let's race Ben, right now...just like we did as kids with no one else around." Ben agreed and we went out on the football field to line up on the goal line, in tennis shoes. Coach Olsen was at the other end of the field to judge our finish.

Trying to psyche him out I told him, "Ben, you know that I have always beat you." He just smiled...a confident smile. We lined down and coach dropped his arm for the start. I got off to my usual quick start and was slightly ahead for the first thirty yards. I knew that I had never been faster than I was right now, so I began to think that I really could beat Ben...knowing, also, that his times in track meets were about .4 second faster than mine. That would translate into a five yard win for him...couldn't imagine he would win by five yards. Ben drew even with me at the forty yard line and we stayed that way for twenty yards when he began to slowly pull away from me. Coach Olsen said that he won by four yards as we crossed the opposite goal line.

Coach Olsen said, "We sure could use you in our backfield, Ben. It's too bad things are the way they are."

Ben looked at me with an enlightened expression as if to say, "Too bad I have to walk right by your school just four blocks from my house, to an all black school two miles away."

And I thought, "Ben and I in the same backfield"...never would have thought that as eight and nine year olds, running in the back yard. I walked home with Ben still making excuses about losing the race...talking about what it would be like to play in the same backfield. I hugged Rebecca and then walked home.

We won our first game and I played sparingly, still learning the new offensive scheme. During Monday's practice after our first game I pulled a thigh muscle in my right leg trying to run down an overthrown pass. I didn't think much of it at the time. I thought it would go away just as other little nagging sore muscles had done all of my life. This would be a game changer for me, though...not much you can do with an injury like this but rest it and hope for healing.

Dr. Nash had a new device that would speed up healing called an ultra sound machine. We tried these ultra sound treatments over several weeks, but they didn't help. I would rest the leg a couple of days during the week and it would feel better by game time on Friday night. Then I would reinjure the muscle during the game, hobble around and accomplish very little. I would begin the same pattern each week during the football season...rest the leg...practice a little... tape my thigh muscle up each Friday night before the game...reinjure it during the game...very little productivity...start all over again the next week. The pulled muscle just would not heal as long as I ran on it the only way I knew how... fast. I had only two decent games where I was able to run the ball well for most of the game and catch a few passes before I was reduced to a hobble. The rest of them I did nothing to help my team mates win games. It was not the kind of year that I expected to have on the football field. For the first time in my life I could not run with the ease and speed that came to me so effortlessly. My speed was so important to whom I was as an athlete, and only when it was taken away from me did I realize that I just took it for granted. I thought that it would always be there for me when I needed it.

I struggled through basketball season, unable to run a fast break. I could still shoot the ball and was good at moving without the ball to get open for a shot, so I managed to be of some help to the team. Baseball was easier my senior year because there was no spring football practice for us. I had a good year hitting the ball and again made the All City Team at third base. There was no track season for me, though. I just couldn't run. I was invited to tryouts with the Pirates and Phillies after the season, along with Danny, Bubba and Leon. I hit the ball well and did well in the field, but the scouts knew that I was damaged goods when I tried to run. Danny and Bubba signed with the Phillies and Leon turned down an offer from the Pirates and accepted a scholarship to a military college. I was told to continue playing in college and…"we'll see," the scouts said. Leon would go on to a distinguished career in the Army…a decorated Viet Nam hero….retired as a Colonel in the 101st Airborne. I received a full academic scholarship to Armstrong Jr. College, where I would continue to play basketball and baseball for two years.

The week after graduation from Robert W. Groves High School, I was selected to attend the annual Boys State event sponsored by the American Legion. Four hundred boys, mostly student council presidents and senior class presidents representing high schools from all over Georgia met at the University of Georgia campus for one week. There we learned about our state government, the political process to pick leaders and to choose officers in a mock political campaign. It was a fun and learning experience. I couldn't help wondering why Ben, president of his high school student body, wasn't there. No blacks were there...didn't seem right. I told Ben about this when I saw him the next week and he dismissed it.

"That's just the way it is...now," he said. Then he added, "But our new President, Mr. Kennedy, might change 'just the way it is' in the very near future." Ben said that "we should talk more about this sometime. There is a lot that I haven't told you." From that day, our lifelong relationship of lighthearted, boyhood fun and frivolity would change, becoming more adult like as we changed into men. We would have conversations more about the future and how we would handle the challenges it would present...the changes that were sure to come.

Ben received a full scholarship to Florida A&M University in Tallahassee...enrolled immediately for the summer session...began working out unofficially with other football players. I spoke to him only three times when he came home for the weekends. He was somewhat disappointed that it appeared he wouldn't play much as a freshman. There were some good and experienced running backs on the Rattler's offense. Ben said that he was amazed at Coach Jake Gaither, the man. He decided that he would major in business administration...not feeling the call to coach and teach high school. I would begin college in the fall at Armstrong Jr. College, preparing to transfer to the University of Georgia for my last two years.

I was very busy that summer also, working a 7 am to 3 pm shift at National Paper as a welder helper and playing baseball for their Savannah River League team three nights each week. It was exciting to work at the largest paper mill in the world...5300 employees, seven paper machines, each a city block long, making 15-foot wide rolls of kraft paper, a Box Plant, Bag Factory and all of the specialty products and support functions to keep it running. The maintenance shop where I worked had about 80 skilled boilermakers, welders and pipefitters along with their helpers (laborers) and those who were in the "apprentice programs" of each of the skilled positions. Apprentice training allowed helpers to get on the fast track to become "certified" in your craft...

more than doubling your pay. Certified craftsmen in our shop made pretty good money, especially considering the amount of overtime pay they got each week. They all seemed to be able to support their families well. The boilermakers' local union decided who would be admitted into the apprentice programs, along with the company's approval. As a welder helper, I would earn enough money during the next four summers, to pay for my last two years at Georgia…room and board, meals, tuition and books…everything. This was important since Mom and Dad would not be able to help me financially. Dad had suffered a heart attack and retired at age 65. It looked as if I really could achieve my goal of getting a college education.

My first day on the job held quite a surprise. Ben's dad, John, was the first face I saw as the assistant foreman led us summer boys out into the shop to meet the regulars. He had spotted me in the line and broke out into a great big smile which he held until I made eye contact with him. I must have looked shocked to see him, because that smile diminished as he looked away. I went over to him and shook hands with him the first chance I got. We talked for a few minutes. He was a boilermaker helper…three years at it. I quickly learned that there were no black boilermakers, welders nor pipefitters…racist union leaders had excluded them from apprentice programs and the company went along with them. Black men in the shop were only "helpers"... and there they would stay...with no opportunity to advance... whether by formal training programs or on the job training. The restrooms, showers, and water fountains throughout the plant were segregated, too. But, after all, it was the summer of 1961. I asked Ben why his dad didn't teach and coach, rather than working at this job...black men don't have a chance. He said that there is where his dad felt he should be...not teaching...that he could contribute more to society there...in that shop... than in an all-black school...segregated from society. Ben said that his dad did well financially with his Army retirement money and the money he earned at the paper mill. I would learn a lot from this quiet, soft spoken, confident man who would soon exhibit a remarkable strength in attitude, character and spirit.

It was exciting as an eighteen year old to work in such a huge manufacturing complex. I enjoyed talking to Mom each day when I got home from work about my day as a welder helper. She would always have a story to tell about a similar happening when she was a welder at the shipyard during the war. As a summer vacation relief worker I was assigned to a different welder each day. Some days we would work on projects that could be done in the shop and on other days we had to go out into the plant to do welding repairs on different machines, boilers, steel stairways, conveyor belts, etc. I got to see most of the plant that way…how it all fit together and how each segment operated…a great education.

The work was dirty and most everyone showered at the end of the shift and put on clean clothes. Three days a week I put on my National Paper baseball uniform and went to a ballgame that night. All of the guys in the Boilermaker Shop followed the games and soon a few of them began coming to our games, including Mike Everly, the shop foreman. I was playing well at the plate and in the field, even though my speed was still not up to par for me. My pulled thigh muscle was still very delicate. The guys would cheer when I got a hit or made a good play at shortstop, and razz me kiddingly when I did something wrong. I could tell that they liked and respected my competitive nature, however, because they spoke of it to others in the shop. I worked hard and the thought of slacking off never occurred to me, unlike some of the other "summer boys" who were the sons of top managers at the plant. I guess they figured that their dads were so important to the plant that they didn't have to work hard and didn't fear being fired. I could feel their resentment of me, especially when it became evident that most of the welders preferred me and vocally lobbied to get me assigned to them each morning. I was there to do a job, so I didn't care. They could think what they want. I was there to learn something new. I really applied myself and some of the welders began to teach me to weld.

I told them my mother was a welder...they were impressed. One of them knew Mom. He began welding during the war in the shipyards, too. He spoke admiringly of Mom's expertise in "overhead welding." I would earn over 1100 dollars that summer and added that to my college savings account. It was a good summer for me as I prepared to enter my freshman year of college.

My freshman year at Armstrong Jr. College was fun for me. All of my courses would be transferrable to the University of Georgia. There was little time for a social life, with basketball practice every day and the amount of studying that must be done each night. I loved it though. I made the team and played second team point guard. I got enough playing time to make it interesting. We didn't have 3-point shots back in 1961, but most of my points came from shots that would be beyond the 3-point line on today's basketball courts. I'm sure that I would have got more playing time if we had a 3-point line. Basketball season ended in February and I got some bad news from Coach Roy Sims. Armstrong's first baseball team would not take the field in the spring of 1962 as I was first told. Money to support the team was not put in the budget until next year. It would be the first time in nine years that I would not begin baseball practice in March.

Ben was home for spring break. He was really excited when we got together for the first time in four months. He really loved Florida A & M and Coach Jake Gaither. He would begin spring practice when he returned to Tallahassee next week... said that there were two returning seniors ahead of him at running back. He was confident that he would get a lot of playing time, though, because the coaches were installing special plays for him on passing situations...to get him the ball on the outside to take advantage of his speed and elusiveness. He was also excited that he would be allowed to run on the track team...both the hundred meters and 440 relay team. I was happy for Ben. I knew that he was excited about his future...doing what he loved...what he was best at...running.

I had dinner at Ben's house the night before he left for school and Rebecca was at her best...grilled pork chops and baked sweet potatoes, with lady peas and her special "made from scratch" biscuits. I thought I would pop. Ben and I talked while we did the dishes after dinner so his mom could grade some papers for her class of third graders. John went out on the front porch to read the Savannah Evening Press and smoke his pipe. We talked about Ben's picture being in the Savannah Morning News. Ben was to "figure prominently in the Rattler offense" next year. It was a good article by the sports writer...painting a good picture of Ben's talents and abilities...his work attitude. I could tell he was pleased.

I went back to school on Monday and so did Ben. He called after two weeks of spring practice. "Man, this is the most difficult physical thing I have ever done," he said. "Coach Gaither demands excellence from everyone...your best effort on the practice field...in the weight room... in the class room...but I love it...know it's gonna make me better. It's just so hard to do it all and be good at it all," he went on.

I said, "If it can be done, you can do it, Ben." Then, feeling sorry for myself, I said, "Just be glad that you can still push yourself to the extremes physically, Ben." I reminded him of the many times during the past two years when we would meet at the Groves High School practice field on Sunday afternoons when no one was there, and we would run just for the pure joy of it...sprinting the hundred yard length of the field, staying together neck and neck during the stretch... continuing our sprint through the end zone and around the whole complex of baseball field and track and field facilities...like two thoroughbreds racing in a Kentucky bluegrass field...slowing ever so slightly from our full sprint...breaking a good sweat...cooling down from our endorphin high...then sitting on the grass and talking about "running." I couldn't imagine us doing it quite like that ever again...sad.

Baseball practice for the Savannah River League began at the end of March. There was no minor league team in Savannah this year, so all Savannah River League games would be played at Grayson Stadium. It is a grand old ball park... loved to play there. Two ex-professional players would join us this year. Larry Hill, a former minor league pitcher who would manage the team, and Lonnie Dolan who made it to AAA Leagues before retiring to the business world.

Lonnie, I thought, should have stayed with it because he was so good at everything... hitting, fielding and throwing. He retired from pro baseball, though...broke his ankle sliding into a base and it just would never heal. Oh, he could still hit and play as well as before, but he couldn't take the pain caused by the grueling schedule of a game every day for a long season of baseball. Talking with Lonnie helped me to deal with my own situation.

"Playing baseball was what I did best...and I dreamed of a long career and retiring one day... going into the Hall of Fame," Lonnie told me. But that was not to be. In a split second he suffered a career ending injury that would dash his hopes of becoming a great baseball player. I had no doubts that he could. He told me that continuing his education during the off season and getting his degree in Industrial Engineering made the disappointment of having to end his baseball career easier to handle...had a good job in the Engineering Department at National Paper.

I really had a good summer on the diamond… hitting around .350 throughout the season and honed my skills at shortstop because that's where Coach Roy Sims said he planned to play me next spring on Armstrong's baseball team. Coach Sims played second base on Barrett Oil's team in the Savannah River League…was good…showed a lot of knowledge about the game. He played for David Libscom University years earlier. After one game that we had with Barrett Oil, he said, "Fleming, I have a lot to tell you on how you can improve your play at shortstop." I couldn't wait to hear it.

Ben came to one of my games while he was in between summer sessions at Florida A & M, making up for courses lost during football season. I had one of my better games. We were playing Hunter Air Force Base's team. Their pitcher that night was Gene Shue, who was pitching for the St Louis Cardinal's AAA minor league team when he was called into active duty with the Air Force. Someone from the air base had a radar gun on him timing his pitches throughout the game and Shue's fast ball was consistently around 92-93 miles per hour. I heard it sizzle on the way to the plate. I wanted to show off for Ben, so I promptly struck out on three straight pitches my first time at bat, fouling off two pitches and completely missing the third. I was getting the bat around on him, though, because one of my foul balls was a hard line drive just outside of the third base line…felt good about that one at least. I made a good play at shortstop for a double play to end the fourth inning and as I jogged to our dugout, Ben was leading a cheering section of boilermakers and welders. With the pressure now on from my friends who were razzing me good naturedly from a few rows back in the stands, I came to bat in the bottom of the sixth, with us behind one run. Runners were on first and second. Shue had walked both runners, so I thought maybe he was getting a little tired. Not so…first pitch was a live one on the outside corner….fouled it back into the screen. He's coming in with it, I thought … confident, struck me out first at bat….not going to walk another batter to load the bases. This time I have to bear down and hit…crunch time.

The next pitch from Shue was another fastball, knee high and right down the middle of the plate. I stepped into the pitch quickly…arms extended…got my bat around to meet the ball with perfect timing. I hit the ball smack on the nose…the sweet part of the bat…driving it on a line between the left fielder and the center fielder toward the bleacher seats of Grayson Stadium. I had never felt a ball leave the bat like this one…a great feeling…knowing that this was going to be a special hit. Neither the left fielder nor the center fielder could catch up to this one. The ball barely cleared the three and a half foot brick wall, hitting the concrete support of the first row of seats, bouncing back onto the field. It was a three-run homer, my first in the Savannah River League…a game winner.

That morning, The Savannah Morning News had run an article about Gene Shue, noting that he would pitch against us that night. There were about 350 people in the stands there to see Shue perform …to win, not lose on a home run by a kid who just finished his freshman year of college. Well, I had never experienced such a cheering ovation as I crossed home plate. All I could do was to look up in the stands and grin, seeing only Ben who was grinning right back at me. The guys from the shop, I noticed, were going crazy, slapping each other on the back and pointing at me on the field.

After the game I went up into the stands to see Ben and the guys. I introduced them to Ben. They read the sports pages, so they all knew who he was as an outstanding athlete and that he was John West's son…the son of one of their own. Their attention was soon directed to Ben. My heroics for the evening were old stuff. They all knew who Jake Gaither was, having seen the Rattlers play at Savannah State College in past years… wanted to know all about the coach, the university's football program, how and what was Ben's role to be in that program.

No one from the shop mentioned John until Bo Tyson just asked, "How's your Dad?" Bo was shop steward for the Boilermakers Local Union. Ben knew who he was...the name. Scottie Thompson, assistant foreman for our shop, was there, too, taking in all of the happenings of the night at the ball park. I'm sure that he would relate them to foreman Mike Everly in the morning. Bo was good at his job as a boilermaker and as shop steward for the union. I saw him stand toe to toe with Mike on many occasions when fighting for the rights of one of his union members... with the veins popping out on his thick neck...insisting that the union contract be adhered to... that Scottie continually avoided following the rules of the agreement on work assignments...that he often neglected safety regulations...made the guys skip their morning and afternoon breaks routinely when work schedules were tight. He called management out when it was clear that they were wrong, threatening to take it to the grievance committee. The guys in the shop loved Bo for that, whether they were union members or not, because they all benefitted from Bo's efforts. But Bo did little for the black helpers in the shop...working conditions... training for better jobs...bargaining for higher wages....didn't seem to care. Bo was a racist, pure and simple...not so uncommon for the times.

Four

I learned a lot that summer after my freshman year...about the work process and about being a man. Many of the men were military veterans who served during World War II or the Korean War. A few of them were war heroes...much decorated...honored. They never talked about their feats, though. The other guys did. As a rule, those who served in each of the wars seemed uneasy when I asked them about some of the events that took place...didn't want to talk about it. It was the same way with John, too, and he was the most decorated of them all. He served in an all black infantry unit during World War II. By the time the Korean War started the Armed Forces were completely integrated, so he was First Sergeant of an infantry company at the beginning of the war...80 percent young white soldiers. No one in the shop knew of John's distinguished military record when he was hired in 1958...the heroic deeds. They just knew that he was retired from the Army...a career soldier... just another black man hired to be a helper...and John, quiet and patient man that he is, let it remain that way.

Then one day they hired Josh Hall, an experienced welder from another paper mill near Brunswick. Mike Everly was showing him around the shop on his first day when Josh saw his old First Sergeant. He couldn't restrain himself...running over to shake hands with John...giving him a great big bear hug...patting him on the back.... dancing around him...looking him over, up and down. John was happy to see his old squad leader and greeted him so...though seemingly embarrassed by this public display right in the middle of the shop. Foreman Mike Everly was puzzled, saying, "I guess you two know each other," John quickly replied, "We were in the same unit during the Korean War."

By now several men had gathered around them as Josh turned toward Mike..."It's a lot more than that. Mike, I wouldn't be here today if it wasn't for John...saved my bacon...the rest of my squad, too." He looked at some of the others now, "What he did for us was the bravest thing I ever saw...took more courage than I knew was possible in one man. I lost three men in my squad on that frozen hill in Korea, but all on his own he saved the rest of us...all eight of us."

Then looking at John, speaking more slowly and softly he said "I'll never forget that, my friend." I was working on a welding overlay machine so I couldn't leave my position, but I noticed that shop noise had stopped...no grinders, blowers nor hammers...everyone was watching John... most of them not knowing what was going on... just something dramatic in the middle of the shop.

Then Mike did the unexpected. "Tell you what," staring at John, "why don't you finish showing the new man around, John. Introduce him to all of the guys. I have some things to do right away...oh, make sure he talks to Bo Tyson." Now, that was a precedent setting event...a black man performing a management function usually reserved for white men. Mike turned and walked back to his office. John began showing Josh around the shop, making sure that he knew where all of the supplies and equipment were located...introducing him to the guys as he went along.

John introduced him to me when Josh wanted to see the overlay machine...saying without elaborating that I was a friend of his son. Then he introduced him to Ray Brabson at a work table next to me. Ray was a recently certified boilermaker working with a blueprint.... back turned to them, trying to decide how to cut a piece of half inch steel plate. It was a costly piece of metal, so you <u>don't</u> want to make a mistake. Ray turned to them, "Good to see ya, Josh," he said only politely, extending his hand.

"Hey Ray, it's your old First Sergeant. Aren't you glad to see me?" Josh asked.

Ray smiled a little more warmly, "Sure, it's good to see ya…been a long time…glad you're working with us."

As they talked to each other about the times they had in Korea…wondering what had happened to some of the guys in their old unit…how they were getting along, John was quietly doing some mathematical calculations on the edge of the blueprint. John finished and laid the pencil down on the blueprint over his math work just as Josh and Ray finished talking. Ray didn't say anything about John's work, but I would learn later that this was not the first time John had helped a new boilermaker correctly design their product by doing the math for them…saving them a lot of grief from the foremen, possibly saving their jobs. Being a math major in college, that part of the job came easy for John and he didn't mind helping when he had the opportunity. Oh, Ray would get around to thanking John…later, in private.

At the end of the day as I was cleaning up my work area, waiting for the three o'clock whistle to blow announcing the end of the shift, Josh came over to Ray's table. I could hear their conversation as they talked.

"I don't get it Ray," Josh said. "You acted like you didn't know who John was."

"Oh, I know who he was alright. Everybody in the whole battalion knew who 'Sergeant Major John West was, what he had done," Ray replied.

"Well, why haven't you spoken up? Nobody in this place knows the kind of man he is. Why haven't you told anyone?" Josh asked.

"Come on, Josh," Ray said. "You know how it is around here...all white. You can get yourself into a lot of trouble if you think any different...try to change things."

Josh looked into his eye, "Ray, Ray! You know what John is in this shop...just a common laborer. You know what a very special man he was to us in the war...how capable that man is. It just galls me to see him treated this way."

Ray said through gritted teeth in a voice that I could barely hear, "Leave it alone, Josh. Think about it. You know what can happen around here if you're too friendly with the blacks."

With a firm voice Josh answered, "All I know is that he risked his own life to save my life and the lives of seven of my men, including you. He didn't stop to think if they were white or black, he just did it! He was critically wounded in that effort... nearly died. He didn't think about it, Ray...I don't have to think about it either." As Josh walked away to punch out for the day, I looked over at Ray...he didn't look too good.

As it turned out, Mike Everly wanted to learn more about John's story...his military career...his heroics. He called Josh into his office the next day, presumably to finish up on his initial paperwork for employment. When they got around to talking about John, Mike wanted to know the whole story…one that Josh knew completely. Mike was a Pennsylvanian, hired from International Paper over ten years ago to manage the Maintenance Shop here. He let Josh know that he was not racially prejudiced…that he could feel comfortable to say anything. Ray began by telling what he knew of John's service during World War II as Platoon Sergeant and then First Sergeant for a company of infantrymen, an all-black unit. He related that John was one of the most highly decorated soldiers of the war…some thinking that his acts of valor were deserving of the Medal of Honor.

He told Mike of an incident recorded in John's Army personnel folder. John's platoon was called to the aid of a decimated tank unit…torn to shreds by the longer range German Panzers they faced in that particular battle. When the black soldiers surveyed the field of battle from behind a loosely stacked stone wall, they saw a three man tank crew wounded and hiding behind their disabled and burning tank, trying to keep out of fire from the Nazi machine gunners who kept them pinned down. John could tell that they were alive, but severely wounded…unable to run…unable to save themselves before their tank exploded. He had to act quickly. Knowing that he couldn't order someone else to do what must be done to save those men he ordered his men to direct their fire at the well-fortified machine gun nest, trying to keep the German gunners from being so effective. He then jumped over the wall and raced to the wounded men, bullets bouncing all around him as he ran. He made it safely and behind the tank, quickly hoisted one of the men onto his shoulders and took off at a run back to the wall. It was a miracle that he made it with fifty caliber bullets hitting the ground all around him as he ran. He fell over the wall…exhausted…dumping the wounded man on the ground. His men immediately began working on the crewman's wounds in his side and leg as John caught his breath. He crouched to leap over the wall again and one of his squad leaders asked, "Hey, where are you going, Sarge?"

"There are two more men by that tank who need my help. I'm gonna go get 'em," John answered hurriedly.

"Wait. I'm going with you. You can't carry two of them," the squad leader said. Both of them rolled over the wall and took off at a dead run, bullets hitting all around them. The tank fire was getting worse, so time was short. On the plus side there was more smoke to help conceal them as they ran. The two black soldiers made it safely to the two wounded men, loaded them on their shoulders and began the forty-yard trip back to the wall, with bullets bouncing off the rocks at their feet as they ran. Just as John reached the wall he took a bullet through his left hip as he dumped the crewman over into the hands of the black soldiers waiting for him. His squad leader's right elbow was shattered as he took a hit 20 feet from the wall. All were alive, though, as the tank exploded with the remaining 88mm shells inside. The three men would have been killed for certain had they been left beside that tank. Now they were being carried on make shift stretchers through a wooded area back to their lines... to be treated and transported to a field hospital for further care. John was sent to a hospital in England for three months for care and recuperation. Having fully recovered after three months, John refused the offer to go home...back to the U.S...said he wanted to get back to his Platoon... that's where he was needed....had some things he must do. He rejoined his company with only a slight limp from his wound, as they pushed on into Germany to end the war.

Josh sipped on a coke saying, "That's all I know about John's action in World War II...second hand information I read from his personnel jacket. But I talked to some who were there with him and they all agreed that he was some kind of man...showing the very best of leadership. When he returned to his outfit he was promoted to First Sergeant for his old unit."

Josh would witness first hand his heroism in Korea, however. John was First Sergeant of the infantry company Josh was assigned to as a squad leader. It didn't take long for John to realize that he could depend on Josh to get the job done, no matter what his orders were...how difficult... how dangerous. Then one day the fighting was thick in a place called Pork Chop Hill. Josh had got his squad into a "pickle," he called it. "My whole squad, eleven men and I, were pinned down by two North Korean machine gunners on a knoll with plenty of cover. Three of my men were dead, two wounded and bleeding and the rest of us just hanging on...hunkered down in a shallow ravine...unable to move...to escape." The rest of the company watched from the safety of a much deeper ravine that ran from the bottom to a point halfway up the knoll... pouring a lot of fire at the machine gunners but causing no damage to them...suffering casualties of their own from the two enemy gunners. The gunners were positioned near the top of the knoll, well fortified. On that high ground they could hold off a whole company of men if they had to. That's just what they were doing. Our company couldn't advance as long as they were on that knoll. John took action. He looked up the knoll, eyes searching the terrain, dropped his rifle, got two hand grenades from the soldier nearest him, and ran up the ravine as it curved up the side of the knoll.

John was hidden as he ran. The machine gunners seeing him only when the ravine flattened out and he came into view halfway up the knoll... running flat out...a grenade in each hand....45

caliber pistol holstered on his hip. John walked with a slight limp from his old wound, but when he ran ...he was really fast. "I've never seen anybody run that fast in combat boots," a soldier would say.

As he ran out of the ravine halfway up the knoll, John took a hard right and ran straight up the hill...right toward the two gunners. Bullets were flying all around him. The rest of our company kept pouring fire at the two gunners, so one of them directed his fire at us and the other one kept firing at John as he struggled up the side of the knoll. Then we saw John take a hit in his left shoulder, knocking him off his feet, but right into the four foot crater that was left by an exploding artillery shell days earlier...the crater that he was trying to reach for his purposes. He held on to the grenade in his right hand, but dropped the one in his left hand as it went numb from the bullet wound. The grenade was lying beside him as he leaned up against the forward wall of the crater, out of sight of the gunners, recovering from the exhausting uphill run. His shoulder, arm and chest were red from the blood gushing out of the wound.

The company kept firing at the two gunners finally getting them to ignore John who was 60 feet below them. That's when John pulled the pin on the first grenade, let it cook down for three seconds, stood and heaved it perfectly toward the machine gun nest on the left. It was perfect timing. The grenade exploded the moment it hit the ground, killing the two men instantly. He slid back down into the crater and retrieved the second grenade...took a deep breath...pulled the pin...let it cook for three seconds...stood up wobbling...faced the gunners nest 30 feet to the right of the first one...threw the grenade. The gunners saw him and directed a short burst of fire at John, one shot hitting him in the side, again knocking him down. But it was too late for the gunners. The grenade did its job. Both gunners flew out of the nest and rolled down the steep hill.

Josh paused and took another sip of his coke. "My squad got our dead and wounded off that hill quickly. I wanted to check on John. He was unconscious when I got to him as a medic crew was loading him on a stretcher, taking him back to a MASH unit in an ambulance."

"John never returned to our unit. It took a long time to recover from those wounds in a Japanese hospital. I was promoted to Platoon Sergeant and later to John's old spot as Company First Sergeant until the war ended. It was in Company Headquarters one day as we packed up records and other documents to come back to the U.S. that I came across John's personnel folder and learned about his World War II experience. What a man he was...what a leader... getting things done...looking out for his men. John didn't return to his old unit when he was released from the hospital. He was promoted to Sergeant Major for the Battalion after the war as the outfit prepared to come home."

Josh finished his coke, head down staring at the floor. "Mike, I asked John yesterday while we were walking around the shop what he was doing here…a helper's job!" I told him, "You're better than that. Why not teach and coach like you had planned to do? There's more money and better working conditions. You want to know what he said…'I'm needed here.' What do you think of that…this place needs him! Why, you can hire people off the streets to do what he does."

Mike quickly surmised, "John didn't say that this place needs him. What he said was, 'I'm needed here.' That's different. Maybe in time we'll learn why he feels that he needs to be here…in this place. But one thing's for sure…it's not money or working conditions."

Mike talked to John a few days later in his office…wanted to know a little more about this seemingly quiet and humble man. Like many others in the shop, Mike had served in the Army during War World II as an infantry officer. He knew a few Sergeant Majors on the Battalion level. He knew that they all were strong, capable, proven men…doers and leaders. In his estimation John fit the mold. I would find out later that Mike invited John and Rebecca to dinner at his house and that John reciprocated. Rebecca told me that all the men did was sit on the porch and talk about war stories...but I knew better. Mike was sizing up this remarkable man.

John's stature around the shop seemed to grow each day. Everyone now knew about his heroism in the two wars in which many of the guys in the shop participated. None of them ever wanted to talk about the war. They knew what it was like... the horror...the sacrifices made...the bravery. Knowing now of the things John accomplished in combat situations made them really appreciate the strong character and resolve that they had always seen in him...an appreciation they had not allowed to surface until now. John didn't seem to notice, but he was treated differently from that day on, because these men from the Greatest Generation truly respected him for the man they knew him to be. Oh, there were some bigots who were resentful, thinking that it didn't matter what he had done...he's still black and he shouldn't be so "uppity."

Resentment also came from a source that I didn't expect...John's peers, the other black helpers and laborers in the shop. Until now John was one of them, their equal. Now it seems that he has risen above them, becoming arrogant. Some of them even bitterly said that he has "sold out" his principles for personal gain.

I didn't see him achieve any "personal gain" during the rest of that summer. I did note, however, that boilermaker apprentices were now unabashed in their request for help from John on math problems and they felt secure to thank him openly. He still had his job to do, but he would often give up his break time and come over to help the newer boilermakers with their math computations. From all I could observe, though, John seemed to be unaffected by any of these happenings, casually going about his duties as before. He had to notice that everyone appeared to be more at ease around him, comfortable talking with him. And, too, John was still comfortable using the "colored" water fountains and bathrooms. He knew that it wouldn't always be this way…just be patient.

What a great summer for me, that summer of 1962. I played well at shortstop for the National Paper team, batted .364 and made the All Star team. My injured leg gave me only a minimum of problems…still could not run. I put another 1400 dollars into my college savings account, bringing my total to 5300 dollars, more than enough to pay for my junior year at The University of Georgia. By working the next two summers, I should be able to save enough for my senior year…looking good!

Ben came over for dinner one night right before he left for pre-season football practice. Florida A & M was to have a good football team this year among the black colleges. I related to him the events surrounding his dad in the shop this summer, telling him the war stories that Josh had explained to me. Ben knew that his dad was a highly decorated soldier…had seen the medals

Rebecca proudly showed him. He didn't know the details, however, of just how brave his dad had been.

Hearing them for the first time, tears in his eyes, Ben said, "I'm so proud of him…don't know why he keeps working there…comes home tired, dirty and grimy every day…smiling, telling mom that he loves it. She has asked him to quit many times. He's had offers to teach and coach in two high schools. He just tells her, 'No, Rebecca, we have both prayed about this and I still feel that this is where God wants me to be.' Don't you think he ought to quit, Dan? You see what he goes through each day."

I looked at him for a moment and then said, "Ben, I don't fully understand what's going at the shop, but I do know that your dad has suddenly become very special to most of the men. They respect him and they acknowledge that, especially Mike, the shop foreman. But there are a few who still don't like your dad, both white guys and the black guys he works with."

"Why do the black guys hate him?" Ben asked.

I explained, "Just human nature I guess…jealous I suppose…when somebody gets something you want, too, but can't seem to get. You'd think they would be happy for your dad's good fortune…they're not…some are really bitter…seen the looks they give him on occasion. Like I said, Ben, I don't understand everything, but I get the feeling that something <u>great</u> is about to happen because your dad is a great man." I didn't know how prophetic I was. Things would get worse for John before they would get better, however.

I had one week left at work before I would begin my sophomore year at Armstrong Jr. College...excited to get back into that routine. As I was punching out on Tuesday, John asked me to call Rebecca and tell her that he would be home five or six hours late because the job he was working on had to be completed today... overtime pay at time and a half...she would like that. He and Carl Ormston, the boilermaker who was assigned to do this job, were bending a large piece of quarter inch steel plate into a cylinder. It must be installed tonight or costly downtime would occur. I did as he asked and told Rebecca.

It was dark when John left the plant at 9:15 and walked out into the huge parking lot for 5300 employees, every parking place filled now with the cars of workers on the 3 pm-11 pm shift. He turned down a long row of cars, searching for his truck in the dim light. Finally, edging between two cars to get to his pickup, he was stopped by two men with stockings over their heads, wearing ball caps. They were big and obviously up to no good, he thought. Backing up, he stopped as two sets of hands grabbed his arms from his rear. Now there were four of them. They were strong...his struggles could not free him...felt the first punch connecting on his left cheek...going down, but, no, being held up by those strong arms. John took one punch…then another…another…on the ground nearly unconscious…boot heels on his chest…kicks in his ribs…the pain…everything black now…feeling nothing…a thorough, brutal beating. He laid there for nearly an hour, when someone coming in on the eleven o'clock shift discovered him as he struggled to sit up and lean on the front tire of his truck. The man notified our on-duty nurse who called an ambulance. John was taken to Memorial Hospital's Emergency Room.

I got to the hospital at 1:30 am after Rebecca called me to let me know what had happened to John…the four men beating him up in the parking lot. I sat with her until I went to work at 6:30. John received a broken rib and a fractured skull at the hands of those thugs…eyes swollen nearly shut…cut lips. He was conscious and had been talking to Rebecca. The doctors said that he would be fine in a few days and could return to work with limited duty in a week. I told Mike first thing. He had already been informed and was on his way to meet with the plant manager, Mr. Lundy. There would be an intense investigation of this assault on company premises. Police detectives were at the meeting, also.

There was a lot of buzz in the shop before we all headed off to our different work assignments. The welder I was to help for the day, Rod Morgan, knew that John's son and I were friends…talked about it before. He told me to push the portable air conditioner to our job site…to the row of digesters, those huge cylinder-shaped pressure cookers…twenty feet tall and ten feet in diameter…made of half inch steel plate. It's in these digesters that the pine wood chips are pressure cooked to extremely high temperatures to separate the wood fibers before they are poured onto the fine wire screen of the paper machine.

One of them needs to be repaired. This means going down inside the digester, welding over some of the joints that had been weakened by the intense pressure that they had to bear. Rod, usually talkative, didn't say a word to me as we made our way through the plant. A specially rigged elevator was set up inside the digester to lower us down, making repairs as we lowered ourselves from top to bottom. It was very hot inside and I was glad that we had the air conditioner blowing cold air through its eight inch flexible hose, lowered in from the top. It blew the toxic fumes generated by the burning welding rods out through the bottom hole of the digester, giving us fresh air to breathe.

Despite the air conditioning, our work clothes were drenched with sweat when that job was completed and we headed back to the shop at the end of the day. As I was returning the air conditioner to the tool bin, pushing it up against the ten-foot high screen wire wall enclosing the tool bin, I noticed Carl Ormston and three other men talking in a closed huddle. Carl appeared to be angry, hissing his words through gritted teeth and

I noticed the seriousness of the looks on their faces...couldn't understand what they were saying.

I overheard several conversations going on as everybody in the shop was waiting for the whistle to blow, and it was all favorable to John..."Can't believe someone from our shop would do this."... "Must have been someone who worked at the plant since it occurred in the parking lot."... "What a rotten, cowardly thing to do to a man like John."

Finally Rod said to me after having been silent all day, "This is shameful. I've seen it coming, though....pure racism....hate to see it." Hearing others stand up and denounce John's beating gave Rod the courage to join in and express his true feelings. There wasn't much talk about John over the rest of the work week. Whether by design or if work requirements really happened that way, most of the jobs the rest of the week were out in the plant rather than in the shop...kept things quiet.

John was released from the hospital Saturday morning. I went by to visit. Ben was there, home for the weekend to see his dad. We sat with John for a few minutes, making small talk, not mentioning the beating. John began to doze off so Ben and I went out on the front porch and sat down in the rockers.

"I don't understand how this can happen, Ben....doing this for the sole reason that a man's skin is black," I said.

"Things like this have taken place over many years….nothing new….maybe it is to you, but we're not surprised," Ben replied. "Like I told you before, there's a lot that you don't know."

The warm September sun shone underneath the porch roof as we talked. I couldn't possibly put myself in Ben's place…John's place. I didn't have a relative or friend who had been beaten for trying to be served at a Woolworth's lunch counter, simply because he was a black man wanting something to eat. No, I grew up thinking that it was alright for all of the black people riding the bus to and from downtown Savannah to sit in the back of the bus…that's the way it was. Watching black people trying to find a "colored only" water fountain or bath room…nothing wrong with that either…that's just the way it was. It's like Rebecca said when I asked why Ben couldn't go to school with me back in the first grade, "That's just the way it is… nobody can do anything about it." I remember John saying that it would not always be this way….it will get better. I knew that President Kennedy and the Congress were working out the details of a civil rights law that would mean black people would be treated fairly…when would it become law?

John improved quickly under Rebecca's care and feeding over the weekend. He told her that he would return to work Monday…'light duty," he told her. Rebecca would have none of it…said he could return next Thursday like the doctor ordered. Mike came by to visit Sunday afternoon and Wednesday afternoon after work. He told John that they had no clue as to who did the beating...not even sure that it was someone in the shop.

"You told me in the hospital that you didn't see who did it. Do you remember anything at all?" he asked.

"I know it was a planned attack. They were waiting for an opportunity like this...me working late...darkness," John said.

"I just don't know if we can ever determine who did it, John. Nobody in the shop is talking. I've asked around as much as I can. Nobody seems to know anything...who might have done it," Mike added.

"I know who did it," John replied..."one of them, anyway. That ski mask didn't fool me...saw right through it...one of the guys who held me."

"Who was it?" Mike gasped.

John wouldn't say. He told Mike that he would handle this...in his own way. John had prayed about this for three days...he would do it God's way...he would remain in God's will.

Mike kept after him, trying to get John to tell him who did it...didn't work....John wouldn't talk. He knew that if he informed Mike that Sam Barton was the one he recognized, Sam would be fired, prosecuted and imprisoned. John would not do that to a twenty-seven year old man who had two small children and a wife sick with breast cancer...a tough life ahead of him even with everything going right for his family...certainly didn't need the kind of trouble this could bring.

John knew the nature of young men. He had recruited, trained and led them into combat in two wars. He knew that they could do absolutely foolish things, sometimes vile things, and be so sorry for doing them the next day. He knew that in most cases these men, when given a second chance, became good men, outstanding soldiers. No, he could not turn Sam in. And, too, Sam would likely tell on the others who might be in similar situations, ruining the lives of these young men and their families...something he didn't want on his conscience. "No," he would tell Rebecca, "I've worked through bullet wounds in two wars...nearly died trying to save a bunch of white guys...not gonna let a little thing like this turn me bitter." She knew her man...she agreed with him...God's way is the best way...forgive... but hold them accountable.

Mike Everly watched as John came into work on Thursday noticing no effects of his injuries as he walked into the shop. John would be on light duty for two weeks, until his ribs healed. Almost everyone in the shop gathered around John as he punched in for the day..., welcoming him back, patting him on the back. A few of them made no notice of the event however, heads down preparing for the day's work. John began his day in the tool bin...checking inventory, ordering supplies that were getting low, and tidying up the supply room. He helped Mike and Scottie with some scheduling and organization…nothing requiring heavy lifting as his job of boilermaker helper did.

The detectives investigating the beating talked to John in Mike's office. John held to his conviction. He would not inform on the guys. The detectives could do nothing…there was no evidence. They would withdraw for now. John had no reason to talk to Sam Barton…only looked Sam's way once during the day…eyes meeting Sam's…Sam quickly glancing away. John's first two days back in the shop were uneventful…as was the next week, with his light duty requirements keeping him around the shop.

The following Monday John informed Mike that he was ready to get back to work…no more light duty. He was assigned to work as Sam Barton's helper for the day in the Boilermaker Shop, cutting and shaping large pieces of steel plate which were to be used out in the plant for safety guards. Sam was cordial in his conversation with John as they worked together, allowing John to do the math computations and measurements, as he cut the steel plate with a cutting torch. John was more than cordial to Sam. He was downright friendly. Sam thought that maybe John didn't recognize him that night in the parking lot after all… that he didn't really know who did the beating. Maybe it would all just go away, now. That afternoon they were taking their ten-minute break, both sitting on the edge of the work table and sipping a coke.

John stared into Sam's eyes. "Sam, I know it was you. Why did you do it, Sam?"

Sam froze…caught him by surprise…voice quivering, stuttering. "John, I…I….I didn't….I….I…"

"I have the missing top button off of the shirt you're now wearing, Sam…the one I ripped off when I went down…why Sam?" John softly asked.

Sam started slowly. "John, I wish I could say 'I don't know why,' but I do. It was pure hatred on my part…the rest of them, too. I am so ashamed of myself. You've done nothing wrong…only good in this place…ever since you came to work here. That's just it. Some of us hated seeing you become so important…so well liked in the shop…all that stuff about you being a big war hero. That's what drove us to do it…just didn't think a black helper should be sooo…."

"Uppity?" John added for him.

"That's about the size of it John," Sam answered.

"How is your wife, Sam, still doing chemotherapy?" John asked.

"Yeaaa," Sam said, letting out a long sigh. "She has three more months of treatment…doctors are very optimistic for her, though."

"Good. Rebecca and I pray for her every day. She put Mildred's name on our prayer list at church, too, the very day I told her of your wife's condition. Lots of people have been praying that she will be healed, Sam…people you don't know and never will know…but they are praying for Mildred…you, too, Sam."

Tears began to run down from both corners of Sam's eyes, "Mildred and I, also, have been praying a lot lately. She asked about the missing button on my shirt so I told her everything…never could keep anything from her. I told her that I was truly sorry for what I had done to you. She held my hand as I got down on my knees, as I confessed and asked God to forgive me for what I had done. Then she said, 'now you have to confess to John. Ask him for forgiveness, too…and ask him if there is anything you can do for him… anything!' Until now I haven't found the courage to approach you. I am so sorry…ashamed…call myself a Christian. Will you forgive me, John?"

John looked at him with understanding, "Yes…I forgive you, Sam. I'm a believer, too, so I must forgive you, as we are commanded to do."

Sam stammered, "Are…are you going to turn me in?"

John looked at his searching eyes, "No, Sam, I'm not going to turn you in. You have enough troubles, so you don't need to add to them. But here's what I want you to do. You asked what you could do for me, so I'm gonna tell you. I think I know who the other three men are who attacked me…Will, Jack and Robbie…got a pretty good look at them, too." The look on Sam's face reassured John that he was right, so John proceeded as if he knew he was right about the other men. "Here's what I want you to do, Sam. Tell them that I want them to look for other jobs. They are all skilled young men...shouldn't have too much trouble finding work. I want them out of the plant within two months...don't want them around. If they don't do this, I'll tell the police what I know... everything. You can stay if you want. You're different than the others. I know that."

Hopping down off of the edge of the work table, John looked at Sam and added, "One more thing...I don't want to hear another word from you or the others about the attack. Let's wipe the slate clean, then maybe you and I can do a little something to change this old world we live in... for the better."

Sam stood next to him and extended his hand to John's waiting hand, "I'll do what you ask, John...thanks."

Will resigned within three weeks, took a similar job with Regis Paper Mill in Jacksonville near his wife's parents. The other two men found jobs with Southern Paperboard, a smaller paper mill located four miles up the Savannah River in Port Wentworth. Nobody ever asked any questions about the young men leaving the shop. The atmosphere in the shop was so calm you'd think nothing had ever happened. John wanted it that way.

I buried myself that fall of '62, going into my sophomore year of college....studying Accounting, World History, English and Chemistry....playing on the basketball team. We had a good team and I played sparingly as number two point guard but I had a good time at it. Days were so filled with classes, study, practices and games that I had little time for anything else. Time flew by. Our basketball team lost in the first round of the state tournament, so our season ended early. Coach Sims told us that we would begin baseball practice immediately. It would be Armstrong's first ever baseball team, spring quarter, 1963.

The team was made up almost entirely of local guys. Some were pretty good high school baseball players. I would play shortstop and bat either leadoff or second for the entire season. We had a good hitting and fielding team, but no depth at pitching. Our record was about even as the season ended. I was tired. The road trips and trying to keep up with my studies were tiring. I was ready for the season to end. I pulled my right thigh muscle again...really bad...added to my woes of just trying to make it through the season.

There was one significant event, however. It happened during our game with Abraham Baldwin Jr. College, located in Tifton, just a few miles from the Florida state line, north of Tallahassee. Ben was off that Saturday...no track meet…so he drove up to watch me play…for the second time.

The game was tied at 7 apiece in the eighth inning with runners on first and second base. A left-handed pull hitter was at bat, so I moved over directly behind second base. The pitch was a knee high fastball just off the outside corner of the plate. The runners on first and second both were running with the pitch because the count was full. The batter swung the bat, hitting a low line drive two steps to my left. I caught the ball about two inches above the ground, clearly on the fly, but scooping up dirt in the process. Out No. 1 was the batter. Then I stepped on second base, only ten feet away. Out No. 2 was the runner who was still halfway between second base and third base. The runner coming from first, thinking that I had trapped the ball, slid into my waiting tag at second base, out No.3, with the ball still in my gloved hand. It didn't register in my mind at first…of what had just happened to me….that I had just pulled off the rarest play in baseball. I started passing the ball around the infield as was our routine.

The base umpire did, though, saying "Son, do you realize that you have just completed an unassisted triple play? The inning's over." He went over to the scorer's table to explain how it happened and told the scorer to report it while writing the game up for the newspapers tomorrow. The team was excited, yelling and patting me on the back. The attention didn't last long though. Next inning our second baseman, Henry Bracker, hit a solo home run over the left field fence to win the game for us. The attention was now on him.

After the game Ben surmised, "You know, I must be good luck for you. The only two games I've seen you play....your only homer in one...an unassisted triple play in the other." Ben saw me hobble around the infield, with my leg heavily taped, unable to run the bases. He knew about pulled muscles...knew that my athletic career was over....so did I. After this season, I would never play a baseball game again. My first two years of college were fun and successful ...transferred every credit to the University of Georgia where I would complete my last two years of a BBA.

I was eager to get back to work at the Boilermaker Shop for the summer of '63. None of the students who worked with me that first summer, two years ago, were back to work in the shop. It didn't surprise me...hearing them complain all of the time about how difficult the jobs were... hot...dirty...physically exhausting. There were 14 new faces, mostly eighteen year olds fresh out of high school. The welders I was assigned to began to let me do a lot of the simple flat welding... made the days go faster. By the end of the summer I would be doing "Heli-Arc Welding," using the more difficult aluminum rods....was fun. My hourly wage for the summer was raised to $2.40.

John, I learned, was the first black man, and the oldest at 47, to go into the apprentice program for boilermakers. I would love to have been in on the meetings between the managers and union leaders trying to decide that call. Once the decision was made, however, there was little grumbling about it, at least not openly. John was proud of his promotion. Rebecca told me so. Around the shop he was the same old John… doing what he was told… helping others when asked…never making a big deal about anything, but developing into a very good boilermaker. He was becoming more humorous, however…fun to be around…being accepted by the guys…easy to talk with…a natural leader. I received a lot of overtime that summer, being the most experienced summer vacation welder helper and I deposited 1600 dollars into my college fund at the end of the summer.

Five

I was excited to begin my junior year at The University of Georgia in September, 1963. I didn't miss a home football game that fall. New head football coach, Vince Dooley, would take the same team that won 3 games and lost 7 last year and turn it around…7 wins and 3 losses, taking the Bulldogs to the Sun Bowl…winning in El Paso. I loved my coursework, concentrating in Labor Relations and Personnel Management. My professors were all PhD's, knowledgeable in their subject areas, demanding. I must be ready for classroom discussion every day.

Most of my classes were in the Commerce-Journalism Building, a huge building housing both the Business School and the Henry W. Grady School of Journalism. I was sitting on a concrete bench in front of that building, studying some notes in the few minutes I had before my next class would begin. Then she walked up and sat down next to me…the only space unoccupied that morning…'what good fortune,' I would later say. I looked into the most beautiful hazel eyes I had ever seen…dark auburn brown wavy hair… looked like Jackie Kennedy to me.

I gasped, "We met…"

"Yes," she said quietly, "at the Wesley Student Center." She was a greeter at the open house for new Methodist students during my first week on campus…talked to her briefly then…hadn't seen her since…wanted to, though…can't remember her name. Looking at my books she mused, "So I guess you are a business major?"

"That's right," I replied…"how about you?"

"I'm in my junior year of Journalism School. I hope to be a writer some day," she answered, laughingly, "name's Amy Parkinson." We chatted for a few minutes. She's from Knoxville. We walked into the building together and parted as we went our separate ways.

"See you around," I said….she nodded.

We ran into each other the following Sunday while attending worship service at the Wesley Center…had lunch together after church…very good conversationalist…enjoyed her company… Amy Lynn Parkinson. Amy and I would see each other every weekend that quarter. It was mainly movies on Friday or Saturday nights and on Sundays we attended church, ate lunch together and enjoyed afternoon walks around campus. I was beginning to see that she was a very special lady…strong faith…a woman of character…fun to be with.

While I was busy with my new life on campus at UGA, things were really busy back in Savannah, at National Paper Corporation. Mike Everly was beginning to see just how special John West is. He accomplished something almost every day to demonstrate his uniqueness among the men in the shop. He wanted to know more about this man who made difficult tasks look easy. Mike wanted to know more about John's military career. On the first of September he called his brother who is a career officer, now a full bird Colonel at the Pentagon, and asked if he could examine John's personnel file…talk to others who might have known him…find out all that he could about John. He informed his brother of just how special he thought John is…why he was asking him to do this…the heroic stories he had been told.

Four weeks later Mike's brother called and told him of his findings. "Incredible," he said. He looked at John's' personnel jacket and found records of his heroic acts just as Mike described to him…incredible stories of bravery. "I was so taken by this. I didn't have time to thoroughly investigate it myself, so I assigned two of my staff officers to track down every soldier who was involved in each action...World War II and the Korean War."

They ran down three of the men who were there at that skirmish in World War II. "Saw it all," they would say, "bravest thing I have ever seen"... "the fastest run in combat boots I ever saw." All of them recalled the same details of John's two runs to save those wounded soldiers who were pinned down beside their tank. Two of the soldiers who were carried away from that burning tank that day were still alive...told us that they would surely have been "blown to pieces" if John had not carried them away from the exploding tank. The Company Commander of John's company, Captain Wally Davis, was killed in action while John was in the hospital in England recovering from his hip wound. It appears that he was in the process of filling out a form to recommend awarding the Medal of Honor to John. The partially completed form was still in Captain Davis' personnel jacket they discovered, along with pages of notes he had compiled from soldiers who had witnessed the acts. These personnel records are usually reviewed when someone is killed in action, but sometimes they get overlooked or ignored. These records probably would never have been looked at if Mike had not become involved.

They also located several of the soldiers who witnessed John's combat heroics in Korea. They each confirmed the details of John's courage under fire on that day, saying, "We could have lost the rest of that rifle squad pinned down on the side of that hill if Sergeant West had not risked his own neck to take out those two machine gun nests." Again, John's company Commander, Captain Jeff Walker, had initiated the paperwork to recommend him for the Medal of Honor and again there was no follow up on that recommendation. It was lost in his personnel jacket. Captain Walker had been wounded, himself, and sent back to the U.S. He said that he had talked to his replacement about John and thought that he would see it through. Nothing was ever done. The completed form was never sent up the chain of command...or it got lost in the process.

"Mike, this thing has created quite a stir around here. Lots of higher ups are in on it, now. It's out of my hands," his brother said. He went on to tell Mike that they have had situations in the past where recommendations for combat medals....Purple Hearts, Bronze Stars, even the Medal of Honor had been lost or were hidden in some personnel file until someone discovered it somehow by accident. But never anything like this...two Medals of Honor...to the same soldier! Of the more than 4,000 Medals of Honor awarded since the Civil War, only 15 have been to double recipients. The facts all check out. John is deserving of both medals. "Here's the rub, Mike. The higher ups are concerned that this failure on the part of the Army to award these two medals might appear to be racially motivated. It would be hard to convince people that all of that paperwork…on a black man…just got lost in the system…twice."

He told Mike that some at the Pentagon are talking about making a big presentation of these two medals to John….here in Washington… President Kennedy doing the honors…at the White House. No final decision has been made, but it will be a big event. His brother called Mike two weeks before Thanksgiving and told him that John will indeed be presented the two medals at the White House by President Kennedy… December 16th. Someone from the Department of the Army will personally notify John and his family.

It was Wednesday….November 23, 1963. I had just said goodbye to Amy as she headed home to Knoxville for the long Thanksgiving weekend. I was loading my clothes bag and books into the trunk of a friend's car as we began our trip down to Savannah…and home. I missed Mom and Dad…hadn't seen them in nearly three months. I was looking forward to this weekend. The whole family will be there.

The car radio was on. "This is a special report. President Kennedy has been shot in a motorcade in Dallas." Details followed and it would be several hours before we learned that he was killed. We drove in silent shock for most of the four-hour trip from Athens to Savannah.

It was good to see Mom and Dad. Dad was recovering from his heart attack very well. He walks two miles every day and takes an aspirin every day. Mom, as she often did, asked if I went to church every Sunday and if I "go to the Lord in prayer each day." I assured her that I was. I didn't mention Amy...too early for that. We stayed glued to the TV the whole weekend...so much happening...death of President Kennedy...swearing in President Johnson...Lee Harvey Oswald... Jack Ruby.

Ben came over Saturday night for a few minutes, said he was returning to Tallahassee on Sunday. I congratulated him on a successful sophomore year of football. Florida A & M's write-ups were always in the Sunday Atlanta Journal, so I got a detailed description of each game. He ran two kickoffs and three punts back for touchdowns this season...spectacular running. He was also used a lot on passing downs...scored twice on long plays. Ben was making his way...happy for him. He told me about his dad. He will receive two Medals of Honor...never done before by a black man. The Army will fly the whole family to Washington, DC for the presentation at the White House...by President Johnson now, I suppose.

I went to worship service with the family at the Garden City United Methodist Church. Our pastor, Dr. George Clary, announced that today would be his last day as our pastor. He would begin teaching in January at Paine College, an all-black school in Augusta. Dr. Clary had a PhD in History…the subject he would teach at Paine. In some of his sermons during the past three years, he talked about the immorality of racial injustice in our community and across the state. He reminded us often of what we already knew, that this would have to change if we are to live out our Christian faith…that we are not living in God's will…that very soon there will be laws requiring racial equality in our society, in all public places, schools, and the workplace. This, coming from the pulpit, did not sit too well with some members of the church. I have always suspected that there was a lot pressure for him to resign.

John's status in the Maintenance Shop was increasing every day and not just because everyone now knew of his national prominence, the plans to award him with two Medals of Honor. Mike and Scottie had both made note of the enormous work capacity of this man. He always managed to complete the tasks assigned to him, and he seemed to always find time to help others with a problem, tirelessly giving of himself. He gained their respect and seemed to disregard his own effort, never bringing attention to himself…a real leader.

After eight months in the boilermaker apprentice program, they felt that John had learned enough to become a certified boilermaker. The shop was growing…14 welders, 12 pipefitters, 16 boilermakers and 15 helpers were added to the

Boilermaker Shop. Mike told Scottie that he was thinking about adding another assistant foreman. There are just too many men for the two of them to manage. Scottie agreed...said that David Walters was next up in seniority rank...the union will want him promoted...the way it has always been.

"I know, Scottie, but I want to do it differently this time," Mike said. He told Scottie that he wanted to give John the job.

"I don't think that's the right thing to do, Mike. Dave has 17 years experience as a boilermaker. He's a good one and the guys all like him," Scottie replied.

Mike acknowledged that Dave could do the job. He had all of the skills and experience and was deserving of the promotion. Scottie reminded Mike, too, that although Dave was a union member, he was very outspoken against Bo Tyson when union demands and tactics were clearly wrong. He would be a good manager, able to make the transition from being "one of the guys in the union" to being the guys' manager...loyal to management.

Despite the potential trouble it could cause, Mike still was determined to promote John to assistant foreman. He called John into his office and, with Scottie present, informed John of his decision, explaining all of the potential problems... resentment of more senior boilermakers...union grievances...work stoppages and slowdowns to make his job tougher.

John assured Mike and Scottie that he could get along with everyone and get the job done. "It might take a little while, but I think they will come around. They'll work with me," he told them. John knew from his experience as a Battalion Sergeant Major that patience is required sometimes when a decision is made which is not popular with a number of men in the unit. If the decision is right, they'll see in it due time.

Bo Tyson, along with Dave and the local union's business manager, were in Mike's office the next morning, telling him that this wasn't fair, that Dave Walters was next in line for a promotion. John has been here only five years compared to Dave's 18 years, and Dave has much more experience to draw upon when making decisions. Mike agreed that Dave would probably make a good foreman.

"This thing is bigger than 'seniority' and the number of years on the job. I have discussed this with my boss and the plant manager...got the guys from Personnel Management involved, too," Mike explained. He had informed upper managers about his plans to promote John and they agreed that John had the necessary experience for the job. It was his demonstrated leadership ability that impressed them most. They believed that he was deserving of the job based on that alone. However, in view of local and national fame and his distinguished service to his country, we <u>must</u> promote him to this management position. It is the "right thing to do"....for <u>us</u> to do for John.

Mike went on to tell them of the Civil Rights Act being discussed in Congress which was certain to be enacted into law during 1964. The law would prohibit racial discrimination in hiring, training, promoting and firing employees. The local unions should be aware of this, too.

"It means we can't hire a black guy and stick him in the labor pool for life. If he has the education and the ability, we must offer to him avenues for advancement in on-the-job training and apprentice programs. Equal opportunity will be the responsibility of management <u>and</u> labor…together," Mike told them.

It was the Personnel Manager's position that National Paper should be ahead of the Civil Rights Law…going ahead with its own implementation of the law…not waiting to be forced to do it by federal bureaucrats when the Act becomes law next spring. Upper management knew that the company's big government contracts could be canceled next year if the company failed to comply with Equal Opportunity laws. They wanted to give the appearance that they voluntarily complied with the coming legislation…ahead of time.

Mike looked at Dave and told him that under any other circumstances he would have been their choice. "I think you know how much respect John has among the men of the shop… that he, too, will make a good manager. I hope that you will support him in his efforts as Assistant Foreman?"

Mike asked. Dave said that he liked and respected John. They could count on him.

John began his job as assistant foreman of the Boilermaker Shop next morning, the first black manager for National Paper in the Savannah Plant. His achievement would make it easier to integrate the plant's restrooms and showers, water coolers and other public facilities that fall. The company acted in concert with the City of Savannah on October 1, 1963 as the city's leaders voted to "desegregate all public and private facilities" some eight months ahead of the 1964 Civil Rights Laws requiring them to do so. Martin Luther King would call Savannah the most "desegregated city south of the Mason-Dixon Line".

Two young black men would begin apprentice training as welders and pipefitters at the plant. "It's a good start," John thought, "Let's just be patient." There were some in the shop who thought that more deserving young white guys were passed over in favor of the two black men… sort of "reverse discrimination"…didn't think it was fair.

With the death of President Kennedy, the Medal of Honor award ceremony would be done by President Johnson. It was shown on TV. John was now officially a national hero. I saw Ben's smiling face on national TV. John would be welcomed home to a big reception and dinner put on by the Mayor and local congressman. It was announced at the dinner that he would be the Grand Marshall of Savannah's St. Patrick's Day Parade in March. It is the second largest St. Patrick's Day Parade in the U.S, next to the one held in New York City. He was the first black man to be so honored. John just took it all in stride, never seeming to get a big head over the fuss being made about his combat heroism.

"Just doing my job...these things just happen...you don't plan on them happening...they just do," he would say when asked.

Part of his greatness as a man was that nothing seemed to sway him from his strong character... good things or bad...being praised or beaten up...recognition and awards or neglect. John kept his same pace no matter what, knowing that God works all things to His good in the end...and nothing else matters. He would hold true to his faith in God and in mankind.

I was eager to get back to school after Christmas break...couldn't wait to see Amy. It's been twelve days. We ran into each other going out of the C-J Building after class on that first cold morning in January. She put her arms around me and hugged me right there in front of everybody...must have missed me, too. She was still beautiful in a heavy down jacket and wool cap on her head. We decided to have dinner that night and discuss class schedules so we might plan times when it would be convenient to get together more often. We would be able to see each other Wednesday nights and at various times on the weekends for movies, hiking, church and dinners. I liked her and she said that she liked me. Things were good. Both of us made all A's that Winter quarter and at Spring Break we each went home to see our families, neither of us inviting the other…still too soon.

As usual, it was so good to see Mom and Dad for those few days during spring break… spent the first two hours just talking…catching up on family matters over coffee and a piece of Mom's freshly baked banana nut bread. They informed me that my sister, Beth, was going to marry George Thrasher next summer and would be moving to Florida. George was an electrical engineer for IBM on the Apollo Moon Program. Having graduated from Georgia Tech, George would have a long and rewarding career with IBM, taking Beth and him all over the world. Mom told me about John and Rebecca leading off the St. Patrick's Day parade as Grand Marshall. She showed me pictures of them in a green Cadillac convertible. Rebecca wore a green dress and John had a green derby and green tie. They looked so happy…and proud.

Ben was home on spring break, too. He came over for dinner once and I went over to his house once for dinner…Rebecca's roast beef with gravy, speckled butter beans and brown rice…delicious. Ben would begin track season and spring football practice in two weeks. He was excited about his senior year at Florida A & M. He made All Conference as a junior, led the conference in combined yards receiving and rushing and in the highest average for punt returns and kickoff returns. The Rattlers were expecting big things from him next year. Ben was already thinking pro football in the NFL. I told him that I knew that he could accomplish that. I was happy for him.

I missed Amy very much…saw her that evening as I returned to campus. Spring quarter was a short eleven weeks, so study time was compacted and time consuming. Cost Accounting, Statistics and Labor Economics each required a couple of hours of study every day outside of class. Amy and I found time to meet and talk for a few minutes each day during the week and devoted the weekends to each other…warm afternoon picnics…hiking in the north Georgia Mountains…church Sundays, always with lunch and just hanging out around campus.

As the quarter came to an end, I dreaded the thought of not seeing her for three months over the summer. "But you have to work and earn enough money to complete your senior year," the practical one told me with her hand on my chest. "Besides, this will be my last summer at home with Mom and Dad and I have a few things that I want to do with them…I mean, who knows <u>where</u> I might get a job in my major after graduation. This could be the last period of quality time that I have with my parents." She went on to say that I should take time to enjoy this last summer with my parents, too, for the same reason…"don't know where you will end up after graduation." It was a long goodbye…that second week in June… kicking off the summer of 1964.

My job at National Paper began on the Monday after I arrived back in Savannah. The maintenance shop looked the same…the work levels the same…everybody getting their job assignments and heading out to all parts of the plant to keep it running and producing. What a tremendous organizational effort it was to keep the largest physical plant of its kind in the world running smoothly…the 5300 employees working efficiently…a tribute to management <u>and</u> labor…. together.

Some of the guys on the company baseball team asked if I would be playing with them this summer…told them no. I just didn't have it in me anymore. Baseball growing up was to be my life, a professional career which would end up in Cooperstown. That was my dream. My future now is to earn my BBA and begin a new kind of career. That's all that that mattered now. I went to a few games just to see the guys play. I didn't miss it at all.

John was busy getting his guys in the Boilermaker Shop organized and working each day, so I rarely had time to talk with him. He did fill me in on Ben's happenings at school. I could tell that he was proud of his boy. The summer dragged by slowly…I missed Amy. We talked over the phone each Saturday night for almost an hour...she missed me, too. I earned 1700 dollars for the summer, more than enough to pay for my senior year. It would be nice to graduate with a little money in the bank.

As I returned to Athens in the fall of 1964, everyone was abuzz about the upcoming football season, Vince Dooley's second as head coach. Many are picking the Bulldogs to win the SEC championship. Amy and I would not miss a home game, and we were finding it easier to spend more time together than we had in the past. She was becoming an important part of my life...knew that she deeply cared for me, too. I began work on my senior thesis, taking two quarters to research it and write it. It had to do with labor union apathy. I spent many hours at the Westinghouse Clock factory in Athens, interviewing some of the plant managers and some of the IBEW union members who made up part of the 400 employees working at the plant. It was an interesting learning experience and a lot of extra work.

The fall quarter ended six days before Christmas. Amy and I both agreed that it was time that we met the parents. I went up to Knoxville and visited with them for three days and met the whole family. They were so much like my own family...very easy to be around...friendly, kind and accepting...devout believers...told Amy that when she met my family she would see the similarities. I went to Church Street United Methodist Church with them and attended her dad's Sunday

School class that he taught. He is a knowledgeable man of God.

Mom and Dad were excited to see me as I got home two days before Christmas, just enough time to do my shopping. But they were really excited about meeting this girl from Tennessee. Amy came down from Knoxville December 28th. She was so nervous. Mom and Dad loved her, as did the rest of the family. Mom appreciated the fact that she was willing to help in the kitchen while they got to know each other. Dad said that the only thing he saw wrong with her is that she puts sugar on her grits. Everything went well over the holidays...good experience with both parents.

I took Amy over to Ben's one evening. Rebecca had a beautifully decorated tree with scented candles everywhere. Ben told us that we missed meeting Kathy, his girlfriend that he met at Florida A & M. She went home to Jacksonville yesterday. I could tell that John and Rebecca liked her and that she was very special to Ben. John told me that the NFL scouts were telling Ben that he would be drafted in the second or third round of the upcoming draft. Ben explained that he probably would be used as a wide receiver... too small for running back at 175 pounds. He was really happy about the future.

"Ben was just as you described him, his Mom and Dad, too. I can see why you are such good friends," Amy said as we were on our way back to Athens to begin the winter quarter. It was our next to last term at the University of Georgia. We would be graduating in six months…lots to think about…to discuss in this short time. The futures that we each had been working toward were about to begin. Would they begin with Amy and me as one?

I began setting up interviews with prospective employers who would be recruiting on campus this quarter. Deering Milliken Textiles, General Electric and International Paper are the ones I want to interview with. International, the largest paper manufacturer in the world, flew me up to Philadelphia for an interview with the manager of the local plant, He was impressed by my knowledge of the papermaking process…that I had worked all over the largest paper mill in the world while working in the maintenance department. He had been to the National Paper operation in Savannah on a guest field trip several years ago, so he knew all about it. He offered me a job there in Philadelphia to begin with, to learn how <u>they</u> do things. After two years I would be transferred to a more permanent location, could be in a foreign country. I accepted a job offer from General Electric at the Space Center in Florida. They were a subcontractor for Grumman Aircraft on the Apollo Program. My job would be in their Employee Relations office… recruiting, work measurement, wage and salary administration, and labor union avoidance. I would be near my sister, Beth, and George…a plus.

Amy had job offers from two newspapers as a writer, Birmingham and Memphis. She had not accepted either job yet. We were together often, making it difficult to keep up our grades but we managed somehow. The spring quarter ended, one to go before graduation. We had four days between quarters, so Amy asked me to come home with her to Knoxville, a four hour drive through the mountains of north Georgia and east Tennessee. She packed a picnic lunch for us to eat along the way, and took me to Cades Cove in the Great Smoky Mountains National Park. It is one of the most beautiful landscape settings in the world. Settlers from North Carolina travelled across the mountains in the 1840's, headed for middle Tennessee. Some of them stopped here and made this beautiful mountain meadow their home, nestled high up in the Smokies. I can see why they stayed here rather than to continue their journey westward. The meadow was about six miles long and three miles wide...mountains surrounding it on all sides...small creeks running through it.

"This place is beautiful," I exclaimed.

"I thought that you would like it. I've always enjoyed coming here with my family," she replied. No one lives there now, but the park maintains the fields and structures built by the original settlers.

Amy and I picnicked on the grass beside one of the old churches in the cove, next to a little stream. We nibbled at our peanut butter and jelly sandwiches, a sandwich tradition that would take on more meaning as life's challenges were presented to us. We talked for more than an hour about our future. Neither one of us could see a future without each other. We had been together for a year and a half and I now believed that I loved this hazel eyed beauty from the mountains of Tennessee…with all of my heart…didn't want to proceed into my future without her. I asked her to marry me in front of that old church, put my arms around her and held her tight and looked into those beautiful eyes that were beginning to mist over.

"Yes...yes…yes," she cried. "I have been thinking about this, too…can't imagine going on without you." We walked around the grounds of the old water powered grist mill and the surrounding cabins. Looking into one of the small cabins built in 1855, she reminded me that most of these pioneers were young newlyweds who ventured out here with their parents to build a new life together…have their children.

I told Amy that I looked at our future together as a "great adventure," too. "We don't have anything and neither of us is going to inherit a lot of money," I told her.

"But you see, Dan, that's the best part. The exciting part of our life will be to grow and build it together...to start from nothing and see where God takes us," Amy explained. We took time at that moment to hold hands, face each other and pray and ask God to bless our lives together.

We informed her whole family at dinner that night. Everyone seemed to be happy. I was thinking that we could be married right after graduation in June. Her mother had other ideas... told me that there was no way it could be done until the end of August...the gown...the flowers...the decorations...the catering...the photographer... the invitations...there's just no way it can be done until August. I called Mom and Dad and told them. They were excited...liked Amy... would tell the rest of the family.

I called Ben and told him, too. He wished us the best, but told me that he would not be able to make the wedding. He had been drafted by the Cleveland Browns and would be playing in pre-season games at that time. They told him that their plans were to use him as a wide receiver and on kick returns. I congratulated him...encouraged him...knew he would do well.

My last quarter at the University of Georgia was probably the most meaningful to me. One of my courses was Constitutional Law, taught by Dr. Albert Saye. Dr Saye was the author of the most widely used freshman political science books in the country at that time. He taught a senior level course in Constitutional Law, the most popular course on campus. He had just finished writing his constitutional law book for that course and the Prentice Hall publishers said that it would be the most widely used one among southern universities when they introduced it next year. He allowed only fifteen students into this class. We all were given typed copies of his manuscripts, stapled together, for use as a textbook, since it was not in print yet.

From Marbury vs. Madison to Brown vs. the Board, the Constitution came alive as this gifted man spoke to us. With only fifteen students in his class he could spend enough time with each of us…get to know how we think…engage each one of us in discussion…making sure that we "got it." I could tell that he loved this kind of interaction as a teacher, never belittled anyone's opinion. He would disagree with those court decisions made by liberal majorities, especially when it expanded the power of the federal government over states rights. He was quick to point out both sides of an argument and never hinted that we should agree with him. He was a small man, friendly and very easy to talk with one-on-one. He enjoyed it when any student pursued him intellectually. Most of the fifteen students were about to graduate, so he and his wife invited us over to his house for a cookout when the spring weather warmed up. I have never respected a man more than Dr. Albert Saye. What a wonderful learning experience it was to participate in his class…a wonderful way to end my years at the University of Georgia.

Amy and I graduated the second week in June, 1965. Both of our families were there so they all got to meet each other before the wedding was to take place in two months. Amy and I said our goodbyes…took a long time…wouldn't see each other before the wedding. I loaded up all of my earthly possessions in the trunk and back seat of the first car that I've ever owned, a brand new 1965 Ford Mustang. Amy picked the color…blue. After paying 600 dollars down on the Mustang, I had 1500 dollars left from my college savings. Amy told me to put that money in a bank.

"Don't' spend it….I have plans for that money when I get there in August, fixing up the apartment," she said with a smile. I headed down the road to Florida…our new life.

Six

General Electric, the fourth largest company in the world at that time, would be a great work experience for me. It was good to work in and see the organizational effort it took to make such an enormous operation run so smoothly. GE had 700 employees at the Space Center working on the Apollo Program and would be building up to about 2500 within two years, mostly engineers and other technical support personnel. My main effort immediately was to recruit the personnel to get the company to full staff. It was exciting to be a part of the effort to put a man on the moon by 1969.

The other guys in the Employee Relations office were recent graduates, too. Mike Shelly from Muncie, Indiana, played football at Florida State...got his Masters in Psychology. He knew who Ben was. "Everybody in Tallahassee knew who Ben was," Mike exclaimed. "My teammates and I would go to A & M games when our schedules allowed just to see if Ben would break a long run." He was surprised that Ben and I were so close. I told him all about Rebecca and John.

I found an oceanfront apartment on Cocoa Beach about three blocks from my office... could walk to work if necessary. I called Amy and told her about it, "It's on the second floor and has a patio balcony overlooking the beach...great view."

That's all she needed to know. "Take it. I intend to work, too. We can afford it."

The summer passed by quickly. I was given a week off for the wedding. We were married August 11, Amy's 22nd birthday....no excuse to ever forget birthdays or anniversaries. Most of our family members were at the wedding, along with over two hundred friends of her family. Amy was beautiful in her "white gown of purity" as she walked down the aisle of Church Street United Methodist Church. We went to Gatlinburg for a short honeymoon in the Smokies...picnicked again at Cades Cove....peanut butter and jelly sandwiches. A few days later we went back by her parents' house in Knoxville to say goodbye. We won't see them again until Christmas. We talked every mile of the way down to Florida. She couldn't wait to get set up in our apartment.

I walked to work every day that it didn't rain. Amy kept the car to run errands and shop for additional pieces of needed furniture…went through the 1500 dollars quickly. It was a great time of our life, living right on the beach. I got home from work at 4 pm each day. That gave us a lot of sun time on the beach…swimming and long walks together every day…didn't get dark until 9 pm. We would look back at this time as the most romantically enjoyable period of our life… no cares…enjoying each other….new friends that we made…taking life as God handed it to us.

Amy took a job with the local newspaper as a writer. She liked the job that took her all over central Florida on assignments…many trips out to Kennedy Space Center….interviewed some of the astronauts. She wrote an article about Walt Disney's proposed new project in central Florida….Disneyworld? State and local officials and some of the farmers who were selling their land to Disney at huge profits told Amy that this project would never work. Disney is wasting his money. "People come to Florida for the beaches. A theme park such as this might work in California, but not in Florida," they would say. Little did <u>they</u> know.

Being a government contractor, GE had to comply with EEO guidelines set up under Title 7 of the 1964 Civil Rights Act. I had the responsibility of administering our Affirmative Action Plan. It was not enough just to offer equal opportunity to get a job with the company. Now employees must have equal opportunity to advance to higher paying jobs within the company after they have been employed. That seems like the right thing to do. The most highly qualified engineer should get the promotion regardless of his race or ethnicity.

That's not how it worked out in the beginning, those early years of Affirmative Action. Ron Roberts headed our Employee Relations office... twenty years of GE personnel policy and practices. When Section Managers submitted recommendations for promotions for our review, we looked within the section to see if there were any "minority engineers" who might deserve the promotion.

Ron said, "Here are GE's guidelines under current conditions. If there is a minority engineer who is qualified for the promotion...if he can do the job...he gets the job. He might not be the "best qualified" for the job....some white guys might be more experienced and have more engineering know how. The qualified black guy gets the promotion anyhow." Ron went on to say, "Qualified black engineers have been passed over for promotions for years. They have been denied the opportunity to advance into management, to get those higher paying jobs. Now, for a time, we owe them some special consideration. We have some catching up to do. So if it means that a few deserving white engineers might have to wait a year or two for the next promotion, tell them you're sorry but this is the way it is for now.

Affirmative Action won't be done this way forever. It will truly be done on an equal playing field someday, in just a few short years. But for now it has to be done this way...you tell them that, Dan."

There were several incidences where a lesser qualified black engineer or Project Manager was promoted over one of the more experienced, better skilled white guys. Section Managers didn't like being overruled by Ron, but they saw the justification. I didn't enjoy sitting down with the white engineer who was passed over for the promotion, trying to explain the company's position. All of the rationale in the world couldn't relieve the frustration of losing out on a higher paying job, one that he believed he deserved. The white engineers resented the "reverse racism" as they perceived it, but there was never any indication that they caused any trouble because of it. And, too, it seemed as though the black engineers who were promoted into supervisory positions performed at a much higher level than expected, becoming very good managers. All in all, it was a good outcome for a potentially difficult situation. An adequate number of black engineers were treated right and white guys accepted it...for now.

I kept up with Ben through the sports pages. We rarely called. He was far away in Cleveland, busy in his new life and his new wife. He married Kathy, the girl he met in college. He played very well during his first season with the Browns…wide receiver and kick returns…led the NFL in kick return yards in his first season…saw him on TV break a long one against the Redskins…Rookie of the Year. After the season the Browns wanted him long term so they signed him to a six-year 1.2 million dollar contract. Then I read that he was injured in a pre- season game in early August, 1966. I couldn't reach him, so I called Rebecca. She said it was a "bad one"…might end his career…severely torn cartilage in his left knee.

Ben returned my call a few days later after surgery. "This is it, Dan…I'm done. The doctors say I won't come back from this one. I have some rehab work to do, and then I'll think about my future after the NFL." I knew how he was feeling…hopes dashed after such a short career…by an injury.

I called him two months later, just checking up on him. Kathy answered the phone. Ben was asleep. She told me that they were moving to Nashville. Ben is going to be Special Teams Coach for Tennessee State University. Coach Joe Gilliam called Coach Gaither when he read about Ben's injury. He asked a lot of questions about Ben…about his character as a man…. would he be a good coach. When Coach Gilliam called Ben and invited him down for an interview, Ben didn't think twice about it. He was offered the job while in Nashville…said yes.

"I had already told him that I was good with it if that's what he wants," Kathy said. Ben would be taking over his duties coaching the special teams in mid season. Coach Gilliam wanted him now, even though he could barely walk. He would begin his coaching career on crutches in October 1966.

Amy and I decided not to buy a home while at the Cape. We knew it would all come to an end soon...when we put a man on the moon. Those five years went so fast. After Neil Armstrong stepped out onto the moon's surface and came back to earth, the great engineering feat was accomplished. The work that was left could be done by much fewer people. In a matter of months, the 53,000 employees at the Cape would be reduced to about 20,000. Our workforce at GE had to be reduced from 2,500 to 700 very quickly. Most of our time in the Employee Relations office now would be spent on relocating as many people within GE as possible. When we could, we would try to help them find a job outside of the company. I began looking for a job, too. My opportunities within GE were in California and upstate New York, none of which seemed desirable for Amy and me. I began looking for something in the Atlanta area, halfway between Savannah and Knoxville. I didn't like the content of any of the jobs I interviewed for in Atlanta, but there was one in Chattanooga that interested me.

I began work at Skyland International Corporation in January, 1970, as Personnel Manager. Amy had gone ahead of me to search for an apartment. She was happy to be near her folks in Knoxville. Skyland was a textile manufacturer who made all of the children's clothes and socks for Buster Brown...since 1901. The main office, knitting plant and warehouse was in Chattanooga. The 10 cutting and sewing plants were in North Carolina and Virginia. The company's 3500 employees were organized by the Textile Workers Union of America.

I reported to the Vice President of manufacturing. His office was next to mine and two doors down the hall was the President of the company... much different from GE...where all my work came from directives from above...from top managers whom I never would see. Now I had the ear of the company's top managers, direct input into decisions that would affect management practices and policy of the company. I had the opportunity to really make a difference, instead of just being a cog in the management wheel.

After attending several meetings that included all ten of the sewing plant managers discussing problems and possible solutions, I learned that most of the company's problems in the sewing plants began when they were growing and adding additional sewing lines at each plant. Each of the manufacturing facilities grew from an average of 100 women to 250 women in just a couple of years, necessary growth to meet market demands. The plant manager and assistant manager at each plant were able to supervise 100 women, with only six or seven sewing lines producing children's garments. Now, with twelve sewing lines, it was an impossible task... resulting in waste, quality control problems and high turnover. The two men at each plant just couldn't directly supervise 250 women.

Mike Jansen, Manager of the Forest City, North Carolina plant created a whole new level of management for his operation. He promoted twelve women to Line Managers. They would supervise the work done on each of the sewing lines producing twelve different garments. He did a good job of picking the more experienced, mature and top performing women from each line. Things improved somewhat, but Mike was convinced that they could be a lot better. We talked at lunch after a meeting and Mike told me that his new Line Managers seem to be having a tough time handling the stress of their new jobs. Two have quit and one asked for her old job on the sewing line.

I spent the next four weeks designing a Supervisory Training Course for our new Line Managers. The course was aimed at helping them make the transition from being "one of the girls on the line" to their new position of "supervising the work of all of the girls on the line." It involved me driving to the plant in North Carolina each week for twelve weeks, and meeting with the women for three hours of lectures, discussions and case studies. The case studies, as it turned out, were the most beneficial part of the course. Personnel problems exemplified in many of the cases studies were identical to ones they faced on the sewing lines every day. In the discussions that followed, several different solutions would be offered by the women, some that they had tried and succeeded at, and others that failed. Then I would offer solutions that professional managers had come up with, giving them an in-depth look at the problems they were encountering on the sewing lines and the different ways to handle them.

These classes turned out to be three hours of lively discussions and debate. I could see them growing in confidence every week. And, too, the women learned to talk to each other during their workdays about particular problems they were having...making suggestions to each other... helping each other...becoming a team.

Mike informed me at the end of ten weeks that he saw a marked difference in their performance. Productivity and quality were up...waste was down...attitudes were much improved...less stress among the Line Managers...better cooperation between the sewing machine operators up and down each line...a much more harmonious working environment in the plant. He wanted to reward them at the end of the course in two weeks with a nice lunch at a local restaurant and wanted to know if I could print a diploma acknowledging that they had successfully completed the course. I had them drawn up, printed and framed. Our Vice-President of Manufacturing made the trip with me on the last day to make the presentations to each of the women...made them feel special.

Mike told every plant manager of the success of my basic supervision training course. They wanted it done in their plants, too. I was told by my boss that now I <u>had</u> to do it for each of the cutting and sewing operations. I worked two plants at a time in order to get them all done quicker. For the next six months I was out of town for three days each week, leading a class in Sylva, North Carolina on Tuesday and Morganton on Wednesday.

At the same time, on days that I was in Chattanooga, I had the responsibility to implement a federally funded program called the "Welfare to Work Plan." It was designed to get hundreds of our city's single welfare moms off government dependency. The goals were very lofty. I, along with the personnel managers of other large manufacturers, listened to the inspiring and motivating speeches by the plan's administrators delivered to the young mothers who had never held a job. The ladies would come to the center each day at 8 am, learning to show up every day and on time. Daycare was provided for their children. They were trained to do jobs requiring individual effort and jobs requiring group effort...learning teamwork.

After several months of this preparation to enter the work force for the first time, I interviewed fifteen of the women who had completed the training and selected twelve to be employed at various production jobs in our Chattanooga plant. At the end of three months half had quit and returned to welfare rolls. After six months only four were left, earning enough money on their jobs to encourage them to remain off welfare. They earned twice as much money as their welfare payments had been. Three of the four women were married within a year of being on the job, now part of a two income family. Two of them would buy their first house within a year and begin building wealth. In exit interviews with some of the women who chose to go back on welfare I was struck by the attitude of most of them. "I would rather go on welfare and stay home with my children than go to work every day, even if it means a lot less money."

I'm sure that President Johnson and the Congress had good intentions when they enacted all of the legislation implementing "The Great Society" ideals of the late sixties, but the result had a drastic affect on black families in America. It motivated young women to have children and to remain single. In 1965 black family make up was strong. Only 22% of children were born outside of marriage. That number would jump to 73% within a few decades, locking generations of black families into a cycle of dependency...depriving them of them of the dignity of creating wealth that could have been passed on to succeeding generations. I could see all of this happening...discussed it many times with Ben.

Ben agreed, "What I fear most, however, is the affect it will have on the children. They will be growing up without a father to establish discipline in the home. No one in our government seems to want to do anything about it."

Amy went to work at the Chattanooga Chamber of Commerce, doing a variety of projects aimed at attracting new business to the area...writing press releases and advertisements for newspapers and trade journals all over the U.S....extolling the benefits of relocating here.... describing land and buildings available to them. I saw her each Thursday as I attended a lunch meeting of the Chattanooga Jaycees, held in the Chamber office building.

I loved being a Jaycee and I worked on the club's community service projects enthusiastically. I became Vice President and State Director in two short years and it changed my career and my life. Selling advertising in the program books of our many projects was the primary means of revenue for the Jaycees. I was good at it. I sold over $10,000 of ads in the 1972 Miss Chattanooga program book. Cal Smith, who managed an AM/

FM combo of radio stations, was emcee of the event. We had weekly meetings as the pageant drew near. Each week I turned in a bunch of much-needed ad revenue to support the costs of conducting the pageant and to provide funding for our community service projects. After our last meeting before the pageant, Cal told me, "Dan, you are in the wrong business. You need to work for me, selling advertising for a living. I've listened to you describe your sales successes each week and it's fun for you, not work. That's why you need to do it for a living."

That thought had never entered my mind. "Do something that is fun for me....for my livelihood?" My attitude about a career was centered around "challenge"..."professionalism"..."education"... not fun. Work was something that you endured for a paycheck, not to have fun.

I talked to Amy about it and we prayed about it...for about two months. I told her that I wanted to make the change and she agreed reluctantly... didn't like the idea of commissioned sales.

I began my new profession in January, 1973 and hit the streets running with my rate card and sales book. It was more difficult than I imagined and sales commissions were lower than I expected. It was early, though. On March 10th Cal sent me to the Radio Advertising Bureau's "Radio Sales Course," taught by the RAB's Carl Loucks, a sales training legend in the industry. Cal said that he wanted me to learn the right way to sell radio advertising before I learned too many bad habits. He had been through the same Louck's course.

The seven-day course was held on the campus of the University of Wisconsin Milwaukee. I thought that I was going up there for a relaxing week of sales training...maybe do some sightseeing. Not a chance. Thirty radio salesmen and sales managers from around the U.S. were there to learn from Carl Loucks. He divided us into five teams for the competition that was to take place. Carl was a one-man show from 8 am until 6 pm each day for six days, lecturing on how to sell radio against TV and newspapers. After dinner we met with our separate groups to work out our assigned sales and marketing problems which were to be presented the next day. My group was led by the sales manager of a 100,000 watt FM station in Wichita, a gung-ho, A-1 type personality. He kept us up until 1 am each night in our problem solving sessions...not much sleep. I learned a lot of "new stuff" that week....never had any sales training before.

On the last day, each of our groups presented solutions to our final and biggest problem that Carl assigned to us. I was chosen to give the presentation for our group. We won and I received the winner's cup for the best presentation. I showed it to Cal when I got back to the radio station. It pleased him. He had won the same trophy, displayed on a shelf behind his desk.

I applied what I had learned from Carl Loucks and within six months I was "top biller" for the radio station, now earning very good commissions. In less than a year Cal promoted me to Sales Manager for the FM station. He wanted me to train the sales staff, telling them all that I had learned from RAB School. The training worked. Monthly billing began to improve right away. Two months later, Cal left for a job managing a group of radio stations based in New Orleans, his home town.

Cal was replaced by Rob Kelly, who was managing a radio station in Indiana. My main problem with Rob was that he undermined me with my sales staff. He constantly contradicted me behind my back, putting too much pressure on a new sales person who was still trying to learn the right way to sell our product. The result was constant turnover. Sales people left for jobs at other radio stations. I felt like I was training sales people for our competitors in the market. I confronted him with my feelings one day in his office. He didn't like it. Veins popped out on his thick neck as he spoke slowly, just above a whisper, "Don't you dare tell me how to run my operation. If you don't like the way I run things, hit the road." I walked out of his office without a word, letting him know that I would think about it.

What was I to do? Change jobs? No, I loved the job itself. I knew that I could not continuing working for this man, however. I discussed it with Amy, who told me that we now have another consideration, "I'm pregnant...found out this morning at the doctor's office." Joy surpassed the misery that I was feeling. We had been planning on our first baby...both 30 years old now...and it's happened. What a mixed bag of emotions going through us right now...the excitement of having our first child...the awesome responsibility of having a child ...and me thinking about changing jobs." I resigned two weeks later, knowing that I had several big commission checks coming to me.

For a couple of weeks I had been thinking about what I would like to. I recalled what Cal Smith told me two years earlier, "Do something that is fun for you." I enjoyed working with the owners and managers of local retail businesses, helping them grow their businesses through good advertising. The "fun part" was coming up with creative ideas and promotions that increased foot traffic into their stores and showrooms...writing imaginative copy for radio commercials... backed by music enhancement or creative jingles.

I didn't always like the quality of work produced by our copy writers, mine being the tenth 60-second commercial they had written for the day. I began writing my own spots and soon became a pretty good copywriter...wrote and produced radio jingles...won two Ad Federation awards. Some of my customers were running, on other radio stations, the same commercials that

I had written and produced for my radio station. They were using music jingles that I had written and produced in their TV commercials, too. Amy commented that I should start an advertising agency, "You're doing the work of one now... might as well get paid for it." That's what I did.

Seven

Baxter Chrysler Plymouth was the first account for Fleming Advertising. I had been doing most of their creative work for more than a year, so the transition was easy. I purchased all of their radio and TV ads on the various stations and received an agency commission from each of them. Within three months I had added to my agency accounts a furniture store, TV and appliance store and a shopping mall. Business was good, all that I could handle as a one man operation.

Ben called one evening and told me that he and Kathy wanted to get away from Nashville for the weekend. I invited them and their two children, Sara and Dannie, to visit us. They arrived late Friday evening. I was excited to hold little Dannie, proud that he was named after me. Saturday morning I got up early and made a pot of coffee, scrambled some eggs, fried the bacon and sausage, got the oven ready for biscuits and started a pot of grits…my favorite meal…knew Ben liked it, too.

After breakfast Amy would take Kathy and the kids to see Rock City on top of Lookout Mountain, then to the mall for lunch and shopping…"Be back late this afternoon," Amy called out.

Ben and I would just hang out at the house all day, talking and watching the baseball game on TV. What Ben really wanted was to talk with me about some changes he was contemplating. He told me that coaching football was not working out for him. "I don't coach as well as I played," he said. "The challenge isn't the same…motivation is different…and it's showing up in my ability to coach…not doing a very good job."

He saw this coming and had been working on his MBA from Vanderbilt University for the past two years and was almost through with his thesis. "I'm not sure of what I want to do, but I know that I don't want to coach anymore." I didn't feel qualified to advise Ben on career moves, but I had the feeling that is what he wanted from me.

Ben trusted his friend and wanted his opinion. We talked all morning about different jobs he could take, analyzing them as to what they might look like ten years from now, even twenty years in the future. We kept coming back to the car industry. Ben had been offered a sales job by a Nashville car dealer, promising him an opportunity to work his way into management and higher pay. Ben could even envision himself owning a dealership someday, knowing that factories were under pressure from the EEOC to develop more minority dealers.

We had a turkey and cheese sandwich for lunch and took a thirty minute nap in our recliners watching the game. We woke up at the same time and looked at each other, stone faced.

"Wanna go for a run?" I asked.

"Let me put on my running shoes," Ben replied quickly.

I took him over to the junior high school facilities, a nice stadium complex with a rubberized track around the football field. We ran a mile around the track in about eight minutes and slowed to a walk. "Wanna race?" I said.

"You're on," Ben answered. We lined down on the designated mark on the soft rubber track.

"You start us," I directed.

"On three," he said, "1…2…3." We ran side by side, neither gaining on the other all of the way down the track…100 yards…looking at each other…grinning…laughing…crossing the finish line nowhere near 10 seconds. We didn't stop at the finish line. We kept right on running, just as we did as teenagers on Sunday afternoons back in Garden City, at Groves High School, with no one around but the two of us. We ran out of the football stadium, across the soccer fields, baseball and softball fields, around the parking lots to the back of the school and back into the stadium… exhausted…sitting down on the green grass of the football field… recovering…laughing at each other…enjoying the moment of what we have always done best together…running.

The women were in the kitchen when we returned, sweating and towel-wrapped. "I know what those two have been doing," Kathy observed.

"Yes, I've heard all of the stories about them running together," Amy added.

"I just wanted to prove that I was still faster than him," Ben said with a laugh.

"But he couldn't do it. I beat him like I always did when we were kids," I argued.

The good natured bickering continued for a moment longer until Amy suggested that we both get a shower. "Dinner will be ready soon."

After dinner Ben and I talked again about our future careers, the one I had just started and the one he was planning. He was happy to hear that Amy and I were expecting our first child. I told him that if it's a boy, "We're gonna name him Benjamin."

Ben was thrilled that we would name our son after him, just as I was that he named his son after me. We skipped church Sunday morning and had brunch together…a fun and relaxing time. Ben, Kathy and the kids returned to Nashville that afternoon.

I loved my work…was right where I was meant to be. Coming up with creative ideas was the fun part of my job, along with writing clever and imaginative copy and adding music enhancement and sound effects into the mix. Advertising was not an exact science. Sometimes I would produce what I thought was a really good commercial and it didn't produce much in the way of results…didn't attract very many new buyers into the showrooms of my customers. And there were times when I wasn't particularly pleased with the outcome of my creative efforts and those commercials had fabulous results in getting people into the stores.

I didn't add any other accounts during my first year in the advertising agency business. I just wanted to learn the mechanics of the business thoroughly and proficiently…meeting with customers to determine their goals…developing the message they wanted to send to consumers in order to position themselves in the marketplace…the sales events and promotions that would boost profits. Things were going well for the agency.

Amy had a good pregnancy. She was the best looking pregnant woman I have ever seen. Our son, Benjamin Alexander Fleming, was born November 3, 1975. Ben and Kathy came down from Nashville and were with me and Amy's parents when little Benjamin came into the world at eight pounds. Kathy was a big help to Amy over the weekend as she recovered from the ordeal of giving birth…changing diapers, cooking, washing, feeding the baby, preparing meals…seemed to enjoy it. Ben and I stayed out of the way as much as we could.

We caught up on the happenings in each of our families. John was appointed to the county school board, quite an honor for a black man when many problems still existed for the recently desegregated school system in Savannah. John is so popular among both races that some politicians are talking about him running for Congress. Mike Everly retired from National Paper last year and John was promoted to Shop Foreman as his replacement.

I have heard religious leaders and theologians say, "When God has a plan, God has a man." They usually cite Abraham, Joseph, Moses, King David, The Apostle Paul, George Whitfield, George Washington, Abraham Lincoln and others as examples of men chosen by God to carry out His work on earth…a specific task that He selected them to do. I believe that John West was such a man. He is a strong man who chose to be humble in appearance…chosen and blessed by God to set the pace for race relations in his community. When John said that working in that shop as a lowly Welder Helper was "where he needed to be," what he was really saying was, "this is where

God wants me to be." God has blessed him for being obedient to His call.

Ben informed me that he was going to work for a Chevrolet dealership in Nashville. The owner, John Bannerman, knew that Ben was well known in the market and that he would be good for business. John had five dealerships in Louisville, Kentucky and Knoxville. Each was run by a general manager who was given a "buy out" arrangement that would allow them to purchase the dealership over a number of years if they were successful at managing the dealership. Ben would begin as a salesman with no guarantees beyond his abilities. He was okay with that...confident of himself...knew he would own his own dealership soon.

My business would begin taking a turn...on its own...with no help from me. A dealer from Huntsville, Alabama saw some of my TV ads for Baxter Chrysler Plymouth at a "Twenty Group" dealer meeting and liked them and the whole ad campaign. He asked me to meet him at his dealership the next week. I got his account and a big advertising budget. After three months he added his dealership in Birmingham to my automotive accounts. It was the biggest ad budget of them all.

Birmingham and Huntsville were both just a two-hour drive from Chattanooga, This allowed me to drive down and meet with the owners to go over inventory, factory deals, rebates and sales goals for the month. I would return to Chattanooga on the same day, work on the advertising campaign that would accomplish those goals and return the next week with the completed plan for Radio and TV advertising. It was time consuming to manage the three automotive accounts, but the money was good.

Amy wanted to be a stay-at-home mom and I agreed. We were planning on more children. She said the she would go back to work when they all were in school. Since my office was at home, she could easily find time to help me with the billing each month. Her role in the bookkeeping area would increase as I added my fourth auto dealer two months later, a Dodge Dealer in Knoxville… still only a two-hour drive from Chattanooga.

I didn't plan on my agency to specialize in automotive accounts, but that's what it had become. I had four dealerships in big advertising markets and all required only a day trip to service them…no overnight travel. I was learning a lot from each of the dealers…things that I could interchange in each of those markets. Advertising and marketing ideas which worked in one market could be applied in other markets very effectively most of the time. Amy and I ended 1976 with sales far exceeding our projections, adding considerably to our savings account. We lived frugally in our little 2200 square foot, three bedroom house. Things would have to change soon, though….we would have another child in

August. This would require a bigger house or an office away from the home.

Ben was doing well at his new job as a new car salesman. He was learning the art and mechanics of "moving iron" as they call it in the business. "The first week on the job I just stood around and waited for prospective buyers to come into our showroom....sold one car." Ben told me. "There had to be a better way."

Jimmy England showed him the way. Jimmy was 64 years old, and a legendary car salesman. He explained his "system" to Ben. Jimmy had a long tray of index cards on which was written a buying history of every customer of his during the past 37 years. Each card had the customers' names, children, uncles, cousins, neighbors, etc... when each bought their last car and what kind of car it was. Some of the index cards were actually two or three of them stapled together as he added children, relatives and friends to the original card. Each morning he would call selected persons from the tray, those who might be getting close to making a buying decision. He would ask a series of questions to determine if anyone in the family is in the market for a new vehicle. He would then call any prospects and invite them in for an appointment to see the cars he had available. These appointments would be made preferably in the afternoons and evenings, freeing up his time in the mornings to continue making his prospect calls. Jimmy rarely took a "walk-in customer". He actively pursued buyers. He would average ten to twelve appointments per week and sell six to seven cars per week from those customers.

For 35 years Jimmy has been the top salesman for the dealership...made pretty good money. When he retires Jimmy plans to auction off his two trays of index cards to the highest bidder. "I would like to be there when that happens," a wide eyed Ben exclaimed.

Ben put Jimmy's plan to work, calling friends he had made in the schools around Nashville... church friends...neighbors...people who knew him and trusted him. And he would make cold calls from the telephone directory...worked much better than he expected. He was popular and well thought of around Nashville because of his playing career and coaching stint at TSU. He would always speak to a man when making cold calls. More often than not these men knew who "Ben West" was, so before he could begin a planned telephone sales presentation, they would want to talk a little football, tell him about their playing days and how good they were. Those were the base upon which he would build his own list of customers, his own tray of index cards. Ben soon became the dealership's second best salesman, never taking a walk-in customer.

True to his promise, John Bannerman made Ben sales manager of his Ford store across town. Al Thornton, general manager of the dealership, liked Ben and when the sales manager position became available, he wanted Ben for the job, knowing of his success. Al has been in a "buy back" agreement with John for eight years. It was nearly completed to the point where he would soon own controlling interest in the dealership. Ben immediately began an intensive training program for his sales team, part of which was the "Jimmy England System." He didn't change his advertising budget and general ad campaign for the first eight months. He wanted to see what his training could accomplish without any other variables.

After two months sales began to slowly climb… four months began to accelerate…six months sale figures were closer to where Ben wanted them to be. Only two of his salesmen were applying the "Jimmy England System," however, accounting for 35% of the monthly sales volume.

Try as he may, Ben couldn't motivate the other sales people to use the system. They were simply uncomfortable pursuing car buyers this aggressively. They preferred doing it the old way and waiting for a prospect to walk into the showroom. Ben didn't want to fire them because they <u>were</u> meeting minimum sales quotas. Nevertheless, he knew that the dealership must increase monthly sales. What he needed was more floor traffic… a bigger bang for his advertising dollars. He couldn't increase his ad budget…he needed more effective advertising…didn't like his current ad agency. John Bannerman wasn't happy when Ben told him that he wanted to change ad agencies. John had used this same agency at all five of his dealerships for over nine years. He agreed to let Ben have his way, so Ben called me that afternoon and told me of some of his plans…wanted me to do his advertising.

The timing of this was good for me. Two months earlier Baxter Chrysler Plymouth was sold to another dealer group and I lost the account to the in-house ad agency for their whole group of dealers. Now I had room for another dealership in my agency. I made the two-hour drive to Nashville early next morning…met Ben and his general manager Al Thornton, at the dealership. We spent the whole day, ten hours, looking over their sales history, past ad budgets, and previous ad campaigns. We arrived at realistic sales goals and came up with the "positioning statement" for the dealership. It was a one-liner that would tell the car buying public what we wanted them to know and understand about the dealership that would differentiate us from the other nine Ford dealers in the Nashville market. To accomplish their ambitious sales goals, I knew that it would require a much larger advertising budget than their current one. To Al's credit, he insisted that we keep the budget the same for six months. He wanted the only variable to be the different ad campaigns and sales events that I came up with. "That way, we can rightly judge the effectiveness of what you bring to the table," he said.

I didn't mind having to prove myself...had to do it before. One change Al wanted to make... Ben was to be on camera on each TV spot and to do the audio for the radio spots. Al wanted to take advantage of Ben's popularity in the area. I thought that was a good idea, too...with some reservations.

I went back to Chattanooga and got started on the campaign that I would present to them next week. The campaign would appeal primarily to those car buyers who had already made up their mind that they were going to buy a Ford car, truck or van...not Chevy, not Chrysler...they wanted a Ford. The objective was to persuade them to buy their Ford at Al Thornton Ford, not at one of the other nine local Ford dealers...by offering them the lowest price...guaranteed. I planned a major sales event each month that would be two weeks in duration. I would spend the entire TV and radio budget during that two week period. We didn't have enough money to spread out over a whole month. Ben would do the audio for all commercials, ending each one with the positioning statement, "If you're looking for a new Ford...you'll get the lowest price.... guaranteed at Al Thornton Ford."

The reservations I had about Ben cutting all of our spots on camera came from my experience with two other dealer/owners who wanted to cut their own spots…wanted to see themselves on TV…hear themselves on the radio…loved it when someone at the country club said to them, "Hey, I saw you on TV last night." After cutting their first commercial in the TV studio and seeing themselves in the replay, each dealer was disappointed in how they looked and how they sounded. They were embarrassed…didn't want to run the spot. Each wanted to do it over, using a professional announcer. I didn't give up on them, however, and after a few practice sessions of doing dummy commercials on camera, letting them see themselves each time… facial expressions… posture…walking while talking…voice inflection. With a little work they improved to the point that they were proud to run their own commercials.

I worked with Ben for two weeks at a TV studio before he was comfortable seeing himself on camera. Ben had a conversational tone to his voice that needed no coaching. The commercials soon had the relaxed appearance of someone inviting you into their home, not a professional announcer "talking at you." Al was pleased with the quality of the commercials and so was Ben. The ad campaign began to work immediately…increased floor traffic…higher closing ratio…more sales. After four months Al let Ben increase the advertising budget to the monthly figures that I suggested in my proposal to them. Monthly sales quickly increased to the levels that Al wanted. Now he could complete his buy-back agreement with Bannerman and have complete control of his dealership. As soon as Al became the dealer principal, he promoted Ben to general manager of the dealership. Ben let me know quickly that he would still be doing all of the advertising, with me as his advisor.

On September 21, 1977 our little girl was born...Geneva Lynn Fleming. Amy again went through a very good pregnancy...felt great the whole time. Three weeks prior to her birth little Benjamin was baptized in our Methodist tradition of infant baptism. Ben, Kathy and their children stood with us at the altar. Being a Baptist, Ben questioned our way of "sprinkling." I told him what my mother told me when I was asked the same question by one of my Baptist friends in elementary school, "You don't need to be immersed completely in water to be baptized. Jesus has the power to cleanse you of all sins with just one little drop of water."

Kathy took the kids back to Nashville Sunday afternoon. School began for them Monday morning. Ben stayed over with us because he was the guest speaker at the fall kickoff luncheon meeting of the Chattanooga Quarterback Club on Monday. Of course he talked football. It was a combination of serious discourse and funny stories of his playing and coaching career...talked about coaches Gaither and Gilliam a lot. He did well... like a professional speechmaker...no notes...received a nice applause when it was over. Many of the members stayed around for nearly an hour asking Ben questions...didn't seem to be in any hurry to get back to their work. Ben was happy to have been so well received.

Things got pretty routine for me, only four accounts to manage. It required only eight day trips per month with no overnight travel. I did all of my creative work and media buying on those free days Monday through Friday...no weekend work. I was able to help Amy with the kids so that she could have a little time for herself...even shopping without having to cart the kids around with her. We were having a lot of quality time together as a family and we both loved it. Life was good.

We took the kids to Sunday school and church with us every week...seldom missed. Amy and I were asked by the Preacher and church leaders to work on various committees but we simply said "not at this time." We loved our very active church and loved our Sunday school class, but, after much prayer, neither of us felt that we could afford the time away from our family requirements. 1977 ended with a higher profit than ever and we added significantly to our savings account.

Ben called me in February with some interesting news. The Ford Motor Company was planning to add another dealership in the Chattanooga market. Construction had already begun at a site in the Eastern edge of the county. They wanted a minority owned dealership if possible. John Bannerman made a bid for the dealership with

Ben projected as general manager in a "buy back" arrangement…very appealing to the decision makers at Ford. This would give Ben what he really wanted, his own dealership. He would learn of Ford's decision sometime in March. Ben and Kathy moving to Chattanooga…neighbors…now that's something to think about.

Eight

I was elated when Ben told me that Ford had accepted John's bid to become the dealer in their new Chattanooga location. He and Kathy had lived frugally since his professional football days, so he had some money to invest in the new dealership, making his "buy back" terms with John Bannerman more attainable. This was a total commitment for him and Kathy. They began making plans immediately to move to Chattanooga. Kathy remained in Nashville with the children until the school year ended June 2nd. Ben would live with Amy and me until they found a house, giving him and me many bonus hours each evening to discuss his new business. Kathy came down each weekend during April and May to look for a place to live.

This time was hard on Ben...supervising the construction of the new facilities...hiring and training a new staff...setting up his service department...and installing a new computer system. On top of this he was required to go to Ford's home office in Detroit one week out of each month to attend Dealer School, an intensive training program for prospective new Ford dealers. Here he learned all that he needed to know to be a successful Ford dealer. When they erected the big Ford blue oval sign in front of his dealership with his name underneath...and on the front of the showroom a big "Ben West Ford" in illuminated Ford blue, he looked at me with that big "Ben grin" and tears in his eyes. "Who would have thunk it?" he stated. In my happiness for him, I hugged him and almost knocked us into a construction ditch that was nearby.

"Yeaaaah, nice move...for a poor kid from the housing projects of Savannah," I affirmed.

With construction completed, the office equipped with computers and furniture, the service department complete with the latest diagnostic and repair machinery, all personnel hired and trained in Ben's way, the Grand Opening was held on August 4, 1978. Ben West Ford was open for business. The Mayor of Chattanooga, local and state politicians and the Governor, a friend of John Bannerman's, were on hand to celebrate the first minority-owned Ford dealership in Tennessee, as were several top executives of Ford. The Grand Opening Sale was a terrific success...exceeded all of our expectations.

Ben and I soon settled into the nuts and bolts of promoting his dealership. He hired Tommy Crowell as his sales manager. Tommy, 46 years old, was an experienced sales manager. He managed a Chevy dealership and then a Ford dealership for the past eleven years. Ben would serve as his own general manager for a while, controlling his advertising and cutting all of his radio and TV commercials. Eventually he would delegate the advertising to Tommy…when he was certain that Tommy completely understood what Ben wanted to convey to Chattanooga's car buying customers. Ben would always cut his own spots, however, putting a personal face on his message.

I was saddened when Beth called August 27 to inform me that Dad had died suddenly of a stroke…84 years old. We had visited two months earlier on a weekend and Dad looked fine …energetic…his usual fun loving and playful humor in full display. Amy and I took the kids to Savannah for the funeral. Ben, Kathy and their kids were there, too. My whole family was there for three days so, despite the sadness, we enjoyed the time to catch up on all of the happenings of each family. Rebecca and John were a big help to Mom during her time of grief. She cooked and took care of all household activities for Mom. John ran the many errands that were necessary. Mom still had a special place in Rebecca's heart.

Ben and Kathy bought a new house in a really nice area near the dealership…4,200 square feet…four bedrooms and three full baths….hardwood floors downstairs, carpet upstairs. "And it's near the mall," Kathy said. She asked Amy to help decorate the house…choose colors, drapes, area rugs, accents, bedding and some fill-in furniture. Kathy was appreciative of Amy's advice…right up her alley…fun for her. They spent almost every day together for a few weeks …enjoying each other…getting to be closer friends…not just the <u>wives</u> of two best friends. It seems that they were always giggling and laughing over fabric spread out on the floor. Ben and I ate a lot of pizza those days. They worked diligently to get the job done. Kathy was to begin a new job as a CPA in a local accounting firm in eight weeks.

One night Amy came home from Kathy's after hanging some drapes…very tired but contented. The kids were in bed. "I want a larger house," she said, not looking directly at me, but off somewhere in the distance. After seeing Kathy's new spacious home, our little 2200 square foot house seemed so small…cramped. "The kids shouldn't have to share a bedroom …should have their own room to grow up in," she added.

I told her that I could move my office out of the house and rent a small office…one of the kids could move in there. But for many reasons, she explained that simply would not do….nooo, nooo….we simply needed a larger house at this point in our lives. "Besides, I think it is great having your office in our home. It's so convenient if I happen to need you for a few minutes for something, plus, when the kids start to school in a few years, you can be here for them in the afternoon when they get home if I need to be out for some reason…happens all of the time." She explained, looking at me for agreement.

I looked at her looking askance at me….and I finally got it. There comes a time in every woman's life when she determines, "Now is the time I want that dream house. I don't want to continue living in the house that I settled for because of our beginning financial condition. I want the house that our kids will grow up in….the one that they will bring our grandchildren to one day and proudly tell them that this is where they grew up…the one that we will grow old in and live out our days…a home that, thirty or forty years from now, will still be the same in a world that is constantly changing…something stable…solid…tradition." A new house…it would be no other way.

"Let's do it!" I yelled.

Suddenly turning her gaze to me, she smiled. "Do you mean it?" she asked, knowing the answer.

"Of course…that's why we have all of that money saved up, isn't it?" I replied.

Amy began right away…looking at house plans…going to "open house" showings by realtors…checking out the different neighborhood developments. We settled on a new subdivision… had plans drawn up for the house we wanted… contracted with a builder and got the financing that we needed by the end of 1978. Ben and Kathy were disappointed that we didn't build near them. They were on the opposite side of the county from our present home. Amy and I were really happy with our church and the community of Hixson and didn't want to leave the area. We were only a twenty-minute drive to Ben and Kathy's, so it was not a big deal. Construction was begun in January and we moved into it in May. Amy did almost all of the work with the builder since I was so busy with the agency.

When I asked Amy why she wanted four bedrooms in addition to our master suite, she said with a smile, "Why, for our next two children, of course. You know that we've always wanted a big family." I remembered that we had talked about having two boys and two girls a few years earlier, but I hadn't thought of it recently. "And you know, Dan, that we have talked about adopting two children." I recalled our earlier conversations that if we were able to increase our family, that we would like to do it through adoption. Amy and I prayed about this next step for our family, and a few months later we met with the Methodist Children's Home and proceedings began.

We moved into our new home on May 28, 1979, 3600 square feet laid out just the way Amy wanted it…five bedrooms, including a huge master bedroom with her own walk in closet. She was the happiest that I had ever seen her…something special about the female species and her nest.

Little Bennie and Neva were tickled to have their own bedroom and I was pleased with my new office in a bonus room over the garage. It was much larger than the small bedroom at the old house.

Amy and I got back into a routine once the move into our new house was completed. It was especially good for the kids. We could easily manage our business in an eight or nine hour day, leaving time for us in late afternoons for picnics with the kids, playtimes in the parks, swimming in the community pool or just hanging out around the house. Our income was steadily increasing as dealers increased their advertising budgets. Life was good again…much less to worry about.

We spent two weeks at Savannah Beach on Tybee Island in June…rented a three-story house on the ocean…in the sand dunes. It slept twenty-five people and we packed it with my brother and sisters and their families. Some of the teenagers slept out on the screened-in porch in lounge chairs. Amy commented, "This is more like a convention than a family vacation." It was two weeks of family fun and catching up on all of the happenings of each family. Mom seemed to be in good spirits…happy to be with her children and grandchildren.

The Methodist Children's Home approved us as adoptive parents and we were so happy. They told us of a little girl that would be a perfect addition to our family. She was two weeks old, dark hair, olive colored skin, beautiful brown eyes and a big wide grin for a smile. We each held her and she studied us carefully. I looked at Amy holding her and I knew that we would be taking little Anna Leigh home with us on June 3, 1979. Bennie and Neva were overjoyed at having a little sister.

Ben and I began planning a big sales event to mark the completion of his first year in business at his new Ford dealership, a very successful first year by Ford Motor Corporation's standards. From the third month, each monthly sales total put Ben West Ford in the black. He still had a long way to go before the dealership was all his, but he had a good start. Ben had become very good at doing his own commercials, developing his own kind of delivery. It was still that warm, folksy tone that made you feel like he was a friend who wanted to lend you a hand, not someone who wanted "to sell you a car." When he was approached by local people in restaurants and other public places, he spoke to them in the same tone of voice.

Ben was asked to speak at meetings of all kinds…churches, schools, community and civic clubs…mostly to talk about his past, football, and his business. Each audience eagerly listened for any principles for success that Ben was willing to pass on to them. He always talked about his Mom and Dad, their achievements and the faith that they instilled in him...ending each speech by thanking God for getting him through the tough times.

His audience was always surprised to learn that his best friend was a white guy he grew up with in the housing projects of Savannah. Ben never used any notes and for some reason he always brought me up in his speeches...about me always thinking that I could run faster than him... being separated from me while growing up in a system of segregation in the south...yet somehow coming together and remaining best friends through the years. "And would you believe it, he has been living in Chattanooga for ten years and has been my advertising agency for nearly four years." He went on to say that I had a lot to do with his success in the new car business. It seemed that Chattanooga had accepted Ben West and his cars.

The South was changing rapidly as we began the decade of the eighties. The old segregated South was going away day by day. A new South was beginning to emerge...with a new racial attitude...not perfect, but making great strides forward. While it was rare for black and white guys to become best friends like Ben and me, a healthy respect for one another began to develop in the business and civic organizations of the city. Black men were elected to the City Council, were in leadership positions in the Chattanooga Chamber of Commerce, and were invited to join the Jaycees, Kiwanis and Rotary Clubs long before women were admitted. Ben was really surprised when the Rotary Club invited him to join. He had spoken to them several weeks before the invitation and he had completely charmed them with his off the cuff, no notes speech. I was a guest, too, and I saw how they were taken in by his "Big Ben Grin," his humor and the serious humility with which he spoke of his life's experiences…his career ending injury…his success in the car business. He was rapidly becoming one of the most popular men in Chattanooga. I wasn't invited to join the Rotary Club.

Amy and I attended Hixson United Methodist Church with the kids every Sunday. She helped out occasionally with certain projects involving Bennie, the nursery with Anna, and Neva such as vacation Bible School. We still felt that we should not commit ourselves to committee assignments that would require meetings, planning sessions and projects which would take us out of our family game plan. Both of us would sub for someone and teach a Sunday school class occasionally. We prayed together daily and when we could, read the Bible together, too. God had chosen to bless us so much…and we were very thankful for that.

I had questions about this wonderful God of ours…wanted to know more about the One who had blessed us so much. I began to read books from noted pastors and theologians like R.C. Sproul, D. James Kennedy, Charles Swindol,

Francis Schaefer, Billy Graham and Charles Stanley…deepening my understanding of why the Creator God of the universe incarnated himself, came to earth in the form of a man and died to pay our sin debt so that we might have peace of mind while on earth and eternal life with Him. As I studied the Bible and the thoughts of Bible scholars, my faith grew along with my understanding. Every book I read during the 80's had to do with our Christian faith…hungry for that knowledge.

Our faith in God was the topic of many discussions that Ben and I had over the years, primarily about the Godly influence of our parents. Now that discussions of religion centered more on doctrine and theology, I realized that Ben was further along in his "faith journey" than I was. Ben and Kathy had found a church home three years ago, a Southern Baptist church with a strong black membership among the white majority. He had been teaching his racially mixed adult Sunday school class for a year. He was very Biblically grounded in his faith.

Amy and I really enjoyed the friendship we had with Ben and Kathy and tried to spend time with them as a family on weekends occasionally. The kids got along well. Danny, being the oldest was very tolerant of the younger ones. We went to Disney World during the children's summer vacation and rented a condo together…all nine of us…had a wonderful time. Spent five days at Cocoa Beach and showed our kids where their mom and dad lived before they were born. They were ready to move back if they could play on the beach every day. Ben and I got up each each morning as the sun came up over the ocean's horizon and ran for a couple of miles at the water's edge, sprinting the last hundred yards or so. I won each day. He never was faster than me.

In September of 1980, we adopted our second child, an energetic eight pound boy with blonde hair and bright blue eyes. His winning smile was confirmation that God had blessed our family yet again. We took little Brett Jackson home with us and introduced him to his brother and sisters as B.J. Our family was complete.

In the fall of 1984, with Bennie, Neva and Anna in elementary school and B.J. beginning preschool, Amy was itching to resume her career. She applied for a job at the Chattanooga News Free Press. They didn't have an open position as a writer, but they offered her a job in advertising sales. She had developed an interest in advertising while helping me with the agency…thought she would like to try it on her own…didn't want to share a career with me. She liked it right from the start, for the same reasons that I enjoyed advertising, helping business owners to grow their customer base and increase sales. She applied herself the only way she knows how, full speed ahead. Within a year she was one of the top billers for the newspaper. Since my office was still in our home, I was there every day for the children when they came home from school on the bus. That part worked out well.

My agency business began to grow again. John Bannerman wanted me to handle the advertising for his four other dealerships. I was doing all that I could and would not consider working more on nights and weekends to take care of the increased workload. I needed help. Bob Smart, a former TV salesman, came to work for me as an Accounts Manager. He would manage all of John Bannerman's dealerships. With fifteen years in radio and TV sales Bob knew the business and I trusted him to do the job right, plus, he was a good copywriter, too. I also hired Debbie Masters to handle the phone and bookkeeping chores. She had several years experience in media bookkeeping. My final hire was for a production manager, someone to take our creative efforts to the radio and TV studios and produce the actual spots that would be running schedules on the different stations. Steve Parker had been working part time with me for two years…very good at it…moved right in. I felt good about all of them. All were very capable to handle their workloads with little supervision, keeping my business lean and mean.

I didn't like the idea of an office at home with employees around, so I rented a small office nearby that was comfortable for us all. That meant that we needed someone to be at home when the kids got out of school every day. We also needed help with household chores since both of us were working. Amy hired Charlene Denton from a temporary agency with a ninety-day trial… she was great. She worked from 11 am to 7 pm each day…house spotless, laundry all done and dinner ready at 6 pm every day…great cook… great deal for us. Things were going as Amy and I had planned. We were home every night with the kids for homework, playtime and putting them to bed. We had evenings to ourselves…no work on the weekends, family time and church…kids loved it.

Christmas, 1984 was a wonderful time for us. We rented a mountaintop chalet near Gatlinburg with Ben and Kathy for five days and rang in the New Year together. The kids loved sledding in the snow. God had blessed both of our families so much…gave thanks every day.

It was a good year for Ben West Ford, too. The Reagan economy was improving and people were buying the vehicles that they loved. If the sales pace continued, Ben will complete his buy-out contract with Ford and John Bannerman much sooner than expected. His success as a minority dealer did not go unnoticed around the country. Ben's story was featured in some of the automotive trade magazines, and he was asked to speak at several regional dealer associations. He even spoke at the NADA meeting in Las Vegas, where he took the time to point out Kathy, revealing that she was "the smart one in the family." In each story and speech Ben always got around to talking about his family values...Godly parents who instilled that faith in him...a father who received a Medal of Honor in two different wars...a strong and loving mother who had achieved so much under difficult situations. And in most of them he told a story of his best friend, a white guy he grew up with in the housing projects of Savannah...of how we both ended up in Chattanooga, with me doing all of his advertising.

As a ten year old, Bennie was beginning to come into his own as a baseball player during the spring of 1985. Although I didn't coach his team in Pee Wee leagues, I spent a lot of time with him on the basics of throwing, catching and hitting the ball during the past 3-4 years. He was his team's best player and ended up playing shortstop...and he was fast running the bases. Amy and I made every game.

Dannie elected not to play football as an eighth grader. Ben was okay with that, "He'll discover where his interests lie. I'm not going to encourage him to play football." Dannie's sport was basketball. He loved it and wanted to play it year round. I went with Ben to a few of his games and was amazed at his ball handling skills at that age...could shoot, too. "Where did he learn to do that?" I asked, knowing that Ben never played any basketball.

"He picked up most of it on his own," Ben answered, "...sure didn't learn it from me."

Amy and Kathy played tennis together quite often, both having played in high school. They always took the girls with them to the tennis courts, letting them bat the ball around a little, gradually bringing them along, and teaching them the proper way to play the game. The girls loved it. Ben and I…we ran.

One Sunday Morning in the summer of 1985, as we were leaving church, our pastor asked if I would come by the church next week, wanted to talk to me. We met and he told me of a new Bible study course that the United Methodist Church had designed. *Discipleship* was a two-year intensive Bible study. Each participant had to attend a two-hour class each week for thirty-five weeks each year, requiring three hours of study time weekly. Its' goal was to help each church member to become more knowledgeable of the Bible and to develop a closer relationship with each other within the church…strengthening our church community. Each Methodist church would begin with two classes, led by the pastor and a lay person. He wanted me to be the lay person. I told Amy and showed her all of the literature on the course. We prayed about it and decided that it was something that would be good for the church and for us.

Our pastor and I went to a three-day training session in Gatlinburg with pastors and lay people from all over our Holston Conference. We learned about the content of the course and what we should do as lay leaders, how to conduct each session. Our classes began in September and would meet each week until June. Six couples, including Amy and me, and two individuals signed up for my class. Our pastor had fourteen people in his class, the suggested limit. It was quite a commitment and amazingly only one person from my class dropped out of the course during the year. Over the next eight years nearly half of our church membership would go through both *Discipleship* courses, giving us a more Bible-based church... sound in its doctrine... a family of faith that had drawn closer together.

Amy and I vacationed with Ben and Kathy and the kids in the summer of '86 at Myrtle Beach in an ocean front condo. All six kids look forward to a trip together each summer...we do, too. It was a fun two weeks...days on the beach, afternoon naps, amusement parks at night, plenty of shopping for Amy and Kathy. Ben and I would get up each morning before sunrise and run for two to three miles on the beach...sprinting the last hundred yards as the sun rose over the horizon of the Atlantic Ocean. I always won...he never could beat me.

1986 was a very profitable year for Ben West Ford, setting local records for both new and used car sales. Ben used those profits to pay off the debt remaining on his buy-back agreement with John Bannerman...two years ahead of schedule. Gaining full control of his dealership was big news around Chattanooga for weeks. It was one of the main topics of discussion at local business and civic clubs. Ben was rapidly becoming one of Chattanooga's most prominent citizens. He had a story to tell and people wanted to listen to this man. Soft spoken like his father, humble in appearance, Ben patiently allowed his deeds to display his strength of character and resolve. Ben called me to let me know of his completion of the buyout and thanked me for my contribution. He acknowledged that one of our '86 ad campaigns won an advertising award from the American Advertising Association for its creativity.

The principal of a local high school asked Ben if he would address an assembly of the whole student body during the presentation of awards at the end of the school year. The school was approximately sixty percent white, forty percent black. "What shall I talk about?" Ben asked.

"Why, *success* and *achievement,* of course... your opinion...how you arrived at your position today," the principal explained.

Ben asked me to go with him on that day and sit in the audience. He wanted me to critique his speech, to listen to how the audience responded and make note of what they were saying. The school's auditorium was filled to capacity that night. Every seat was taken with some standing in the rear. I stood in the back so I could move around and get a better feel for the mood of the crowd. The principal introduced Ben as he read from a brief resume of Ben's background and history that I had prepared. There was a noticeable quietness when the principal told of Ben's dad's military career, that he was awarded the Medal of Honor twice.

When Ben took the podium, all eyes were on him. He didn't tell me beforehand what he was going to say to these young people. I had heard him talk to adult organizations many times, so I had an idea of what he would tell them. I leaned against the back wall of the auditorium to get comfortable for one of his thirty-minute orations. This one would be only eighteen minutes of well chosen words. He didn't talk about his football career and he said not one word of his career ending injury. That had to be disappointing to many of the fathers in the audience.

He started out by talking about how important education had always been to his family growing up in Savannah...how hard his mother worked to earn her college degree...attending classes for eight years...how patient she was, finally becoming a teacher at twenty-nine years of age. He talked about his dad's struggle though college during the depression, getting a degree in Math and joining the Army. His dad's education prepared him for success as a non- commissioned officer in the Army. That and his work ethic allowed him to advance to the highest rank a noncommissioned officer can achieve in the Army, becoming Sergeant Major over a Brigade of twelve hundred men. That experience of training and leading twelve hundred men into battle would prepare him to be a manager in the manufacturing business and a community leader after he retired from the Army.

"Thanks to my parents' encouragement, I pursued an MBA from Vanderbilt while coaching and trying to decide what I wanted to do with my life," Ben explained. "I didn't know what I wanted to do specifically, but I knew that I needed to be prepared when an opportunity came my way." Ben went on to say that John Bannerman hired him to sell cars. He worked hard and did that job well. Once in the car business, however, he knew that he wanted to be more than a salesman. His goal was to be a manager or even a dealer someday, with *Ben West* on the sign. He was given the opportunity to become the sales manager of a dealership and he became a very good sales manager. When the opportunity to become general manager of a dealership was opened, he got the job...because he was prepared and he worked hard.

"I worked hard at being a good general manager of that dealership. When the opportunity arose for me to own a new car dealership the decision makers knew that I was prepared for the task. I was given the opportunity to own a new car dealership." He told them his dealership had been successful right from the start and that he was able to complete his buyout from John

Bannerman and Ford in just eight years instead of the ten years he was given. "I want you to know that I didn't do it alone. I had a lot of help from some good people." He explained that he had forty-three people working for him...interviewed and hired each one...sales people, mechanics, office clerks...eighteen are black and twenty-five are white.

Ben paused and looked across his audience, "I hire only smart, educated people. They get the good jobs. I won't hire someone, black or white, who can't do the job successfully if they are unprepared. The man who hired me, trained me and allowed me the opportunity to buy my own dealership was a white man who didn't look to see if I was white or black. He looked at my education and work experience to see if I was prepared to succeed."

Ben went on to tell them that opportunities for success will surely come their way if they are patient and watchful. The big question is, "Will you be prepared to take advantage of those opportunities as they arise? Will you have the education, training and track record that shows you worked hard at your previous jobs and you were successful at those jobs? My charge to you is to prepare yourself for success so that when opportunities present themselves to you...as they surely will...that you'll be ready to take advantage of them."

Ben remained on the stage of the auditorium as the names were called of each student who earned an award. I was astonished at the amount of scholarship money that was awarded and the number of recipients. Ben shook hands with each of them and seemed to always have a few words to say to them, generating smiles and laughter from each one.

What I didn't know at the time was that a Chattanooga Times reporter had recorded every word of Ben's speech and it was printed in its entirety the next day. Newspapers from Knoxville and Nashville picked up the story and it was all over East Tennessee. Ben had created a bit of a buzz around town. In the days that followed there were letters to the editor supporting Ben's ideas about success, saying that he was right. Young people can't blame anyone else but themselves if they fail...not their parents' fault...not the school system's fault and it's not discrimination in most cases.

There were some letters to the editor taking issue with him, too, "Ben's story is the exception, not the rule"..."filled the kids' minds with a lot of false hope"..."monetary success is not as simple as he expressed it"..."discrimination is a factor"... ."kids will lose heart and be worse off than ever." Ben told me that he was not concerned over all of the controversy. At least people are talking about the subject, maybe doing something positive about it. "You know, Dan, if I reached just two or three kids with the truth of that idea and they make something out of themselves, it was a good thing," he said. I told him that from my observations, he influenced quite a few individuals.

Bennie was in his last year of Little League baseball, doing quite well as a pitcher and shortstop. Amy and I made every game and cheered him on. Neva was ten years old and all she wanted to do was play tennis...year round. She participated in several leagues at the Racket Club, making a name for herself. She is already taking on the twelve to fourteen year old group. Anna's swimming classes had shown her to be a graceful and strong swimmer and she was enjoying year round swimming as well. And B.J., at six years old, was finding fun in any activity that was full of action. It was fun to watch them grow up. Dannie would be a senior next year and already had basketball scholarships from several small colleges. He was fine with that. Sarah volunteered as a candy stripe aide at a local hospital for the summers.

We vacationed at the beach on Tybee Island again in that summer of '87, inviting Ben, Kathy and the kids to go with us. Most of my family was there. Beth was happy to see Ben again. She talked with him a lot about his car dealership... told him that stories of his success had made the papers in Virginia. It was a fun and relaxing two weeks. Ben and I did our thing every morning at sunrise...running on the beach for a couple of miles and sprinting the final 100 yards. I beat him every time in the sprint...could always run faster than Ben.

Rebecca and John now lived near the beach on Wilmington Island in their retirement years. They invited us over one night for a visit. Rebecca promised a surprise for dinner. It was a beautiful retirement home, a rancher built with old Savannah gray bricks with white trim and nestled under several huge live oak trees covered in Spanish moss. John was 69 and Rebecca was 68, neither one looking their age. "How's my boy?" Rebecca asked as she squeezed me real good. She spent a lot of time talking with Amy as she and Kathy helped in the Kitchen.

Ben showed me a glass-enclosed display of John's medals that he earned during his military career over two wars. The two Medals of Honor were prominently displayed on a bed of burgundy velvet surrounded by his two Purple Hearts and various other medals and service ribbons making up the display. She gave it to John at his retirement party from National Paper. I enjoyed talking over old times at the paper mill with this great man of God...and I loved Rebecca. They were an important part of my life. Amy wanted to talk about John and Rebecca all the way back to Chattanooga, asking me hundreds of questions...will I sing the "Johnny Appleseed" song one more time for her and the kids?

I had to really concentrate on my agency work. Many new models were being introduced by the factories in the fall of '87. Most of my dealers were achieving fabulous sales figures for the year to date. President Reagan had the economy humming. Even the stock market crash in October, Black Monday they called it, had little effect on new car sales. Ben ended the year with his biggest profits ever. He gave each employee a sizable Christmas bonus. Ben and I took our families to Gatlinburg over the New Year Holidays. There was eight inches of snow on the ground...looked more like Aspen than Gatlinburg. This was becoming a great tradition for our families. The kids loved to ski. Amy and Kathy loved the quaint little shops along the streets of Gatlinburg...Ben and I napped a lot.

January 1, 1988 Ben promoted Tommy Crowell to general manager as he had promised. Tommy was ready for the job. John Newton, a 28 year-old black man was promoted to sales manager, taking Tommy's old position. Ben questioned Tommy's choice because John was so young. He had been with the dealership for only six years, starting just after he graduated from The University of Tennessee. Ben acknowledged that he was their top salesman, but he still felt John was too young for the job. Tommy said that John had a strong resolve and mental toughness. He had learned the business of selling cars very well and would do a good job as sales manager. Ben relented.

Ben and Kathy's kids, Dannie and Sarah, seemed to want to keep Amy and me involved in the happenings of their lives. Both of them were in high school now, Dannie a senior and

Sarah a sophomore. Sarah had found herself in the school's chorus and drama club. She let us know when her performances took place so that we could attend. She had been taking voice and dance lessons for three years. She had a good singing voice for her age…sounded much like her grandmother.

I kept up with Dannie's basketball season through write ups in the newspaper and by attending some of the important games. I didn't miss a game during the region and state finals. His team finished third in their classification. Dannie averaged twenty-four points per game his final year and was a terrific point guard. Because he was just 5'10", no Division 1 college seemed to be interested in offering him a scholarship. He wanted to go to Vanderbilt and had already been accepted by the University. He had offers from several of the smaller colleges, but he liked Vanderbilt. After much discussion with his parents and his "Uncle Dan," Dannie decided that he would attend Vanderbilt and try to play basketball as a *walk on* next fall.

Summer vacation time for us as family would be different this year, 1988. We scheduled our annual beach trip with Ben, Kathy and their kids in June. Kathy rented a house on the beach at Gulf Shores on the Florida panhandle. We ate at a different seafood restaurant every night, all of it good. Ben and I ran for two to three miles on the beach at sunrise each morning, sprinting the last hundred yards. I won every day...never could run as fast as I could. I noticed that he began to limp more than usual after our cool down walk. Ben said it was nothing serious...not to worry.

Amy and I had talked about a driving vacation with the kids out west, for all of us to see this big country of ours. I got the maps and travel books from AAA and planned the route that we would take and calculated the driving time between national parks and attractions that we wanted to see. I determined that it would be a twenty-one day vacation. That's a long time to be cooped up in a vehicle so I bought the biggest passenger vehicle I could find...a brand new Ford LTD station wagon from Ben. It was roomy enough for the kids to stretch out in the two rows of seats in the back. Then I bought a luggage carrier to strap on top, one large enough to hold our suitcases and necessaries for the trip. This allowed plenty of space inside the wagon for games, books, etc. to keep everyone occupied during long drives on the trip. Amy and I were just as excited as the kids, since neither of us had ever been on such a great adventure.

We left Chattanooga on Wednesday, July 7th at 3 pm and picnicked in St. Louis at midnight under the Arch...peanut butter and jelly sandwiches. The next day was a long one, thirteen hours of driving across Missouri and Kansas, arriving in Denver at 9 pm. Neva said that she never wanted to see a corn field again and was relieved when

I told her that we wouldn't have another day like that one on this trip. The snow capped Rockies west of Denver were beautiful. We spent two days exploring them…old west towns, gold mines and freezing cold mountain lakes.

Next we drove through Wyoming up to Jackson Hole and Yellowstone. Amy and the kids allowed me just three hours at the Old West Museum in Cheyenne…could have spent three days. Jackson Hole and the Grand Teton Mountains were breathtaking, seeing them for the first time. We stayed at the Jackson Lake Lodge…beautifully rustic at the foot of the mountain range, overlooking Jackson Lake. I woke up just before sunrise on the first morning and went down to the lobby for coffee. The lobby was sixty feet across and three floors high, with huge windows covering the entire wall from floor to ceiling, looking out across the lake to the Tetons. As the sun came up, the granite gray mountains slowly took on a golden glow, giving them the appearance of massive nuggets of gold. It was a beautiful sight…a worshipful experience. I sat in one of the chairs looking out the window and prayed, thanking God for His wonderful creation.

Yellowstone National Park was a home run for the kids. B.J. had made a list of the animals he wanted to see and was checking them off as we came upon them. We spent two nights at the Old Faithful Inn, next to the fabled geyser. The scenery is magnificent...rivers and waterfalls, canyons and hot springs and lots of animals.

As we were leaving the park, I looked in my rear view mirror and I noticed that B.J. had a frown of disappointment on his face. I asked him what was wrong. "Daddy, I have seen all of the animals on my list except a bear...and that's the one I really wanted to see," he said, disappointment in his voice. I quickly offered a silent prayer for that to happen as I drove the wagon. I rounded a curve in the road and the hills opened up into a large grassy meadow... several cars pulled over to the side.... people with binoculars looking at something.

"A bear," I yelled to B.J. and pulled over to the side of the road, too.

The huge black bear was about a hundred yards out in the meadow, eating something on an old log he had overturned by the bank of the river that was between him and us. We took a few pictures of B.J. with the bear in the background... he was happy. I told Amy of my prayer and she reminded me that no prayer is too big or too small for God...He answers them all...in His own time. This one was quick. We drove into Montana and Glacier National Park...beautiful...hope the glaciers never melt. We spent the night in the old rustic McDonald Lake Lodge on the western side of the park. We drove through Montana, Idaho, and eastern Washington to Hoover Dam. The kids enjoyed the tour of this engineering feat as much as Amy and I. Next day we drove across the Cascade Mountains into Seattle, where we visited with Amy's brother Jack, an engineer with a company that had a subcontract with Boeing. Jack showed us the sights around Seattle, took us to Mt. Rainier and out on his 32-foot boat into Puget Sound. Saying goodbye was hard for Amy. She sees Jack so infrequently because of the distance.

After driving through Oregon, The Lewis and Clark sites, the Willamette Valley, Mt. Hood and Crater Lake, we drove down the middle of California, taking in the scenery of the wine country in Napa Valley, sampling some of the wine. Leaving Napa Valley, we drove straight to the Pacific Ocean and frolicked on the beach, barefooted in our Bermuda shorts…our first dip in the Pacific Ocean. We crossed the Golden Gate Bridge late that afternoon for two days in San Francisco. Amy, Neva and Anna wanted to stay in San Francisco an extra day, tightening our schedule for the rest of the trip but it was worth it.

Next, we visited Yosemite Park, one of the most picturesque natural settings you'll ever see…the sheer wall of El Capitan, the huge waterfall and the river flowing through the valley. Next day we drove down to the Sequoia Forest. The world's largest trees were spectacular. We were behind schedule, so I made it a long driving day as we left the great trees. It was 10 pm when we checked into a motel in the middle of the Mojave Desert. It was still 104 degrees. The kids wanted to go swimming before bedtime but the pool closed at 9 pm. I convinced the motel owner that we would assume all responsibility, so he allowed us the use of the pool.

I let everyone sleep late next morning while I went down for breakfast, coffee and the L.A. Times. The world was operating very well without us, it seems. We drove across the desert to the Grand Canyon and watched one of the most beautiful sunsets you'll ever see. We then went through the Navajo Indian Reservation and visited a few ruins of ancient adobe brick villages. I had planned to spend a couple of days in the Santa Fe area, but time didn't allow it. We hurried through the Texas panhandle, Oklahoma and Arkansas to get back to Chattanooga on July 28, the 21st day. It was a great vacation for all of us, a learning experience of our great country that you just can't get any other way...a family event that none of us will ever forget.

Ben called on my first day back from vacation. He wanted me to meet with him and City Councilman, Jason Benton, in his office at the dealership. Jason was running as a Republican candidate for the U.S. House of Representatives against the Democrat incumbent. Ben was on his election campaign committee and was the campaign treasurer. For some reason that they didn't explain, the campaign had dumped the advertising firm that they used during the primary. The polls showed that Jason now trailed the incumbent by double digits. Ben strongly suggested me as the replacement. As busy as I was with all of the "model year-end sales" going on at each of my dealerships, I agreed to handle that chore for them.

Ben left the management of his dealership almost entirely to Tommy Crowell while campaigning for Jason. This was my first attempt at speechwriting for a politician, not too much different from writing a sixty-second radio commercial. Ben was all over the congressional district campaigning for Jason, giving speeches to civic clubs, churches, businesses and various kinds of organizations. He even attended small neighborhood coffees during morning hours, usually attended by eight to fifteen women organized by campaign volunteers. Ben fired up the crowd wherever he went, with his "Big Ben Grin" and folksy, homespun humor, showing to all that, like Jason, he, too, was a Christian conservative. "If people of faith don't run for political office, can we ever expect to have a government that will do the right thing for its people?" he exclaimed with passion. Ben endeared himself to everyone he met on the campaign trail.

Polls taken on the first week in November showed that we had closed the gap quite a bit. The incumbent was still ahead but only by two points. It was a tossup now. Jason lost by three points and we were disappointed but one thing was certain…Ben and I had a big time. We enjoyed the competition.

I had lunch with Ed Germaine, local chairman of the Republican Party, a week after the election. He said that most GOP leaders had concluded that they wanted Ben to run for Congress in two years. They had all been present for at least one of his speeches on behalf of Jason during the recent campaign. Ben impressed them so much… his conservative principles of a smaller, less costly government…being a good steward of the taxpayers' money…his faith in God that he so comfortably proclaimed …always speaking off the cuff with no notes…his ability to wow a crowd with his smile and his easy going nature, no matter what the makeup of the crowd..

Their question for me was one of marketing and advertising. Could a black man be elected to congress from this district? It hasn't been done before. My answer was yes. Ben was one of the most popular men in the community. He has sold himself to the Chattanooga market through his dealership's TV and radio advertising over the past ten years, making his dealership one of the most successful new car operations in the state. New car buyers have come to his dealership from as far away as a hundred miles to buy a Ford from Ben…because he told them that he would give them a lower price. His face was more identifiable to Chattanoogans than that of Ronald Reagan. "Yes, he can be elected," I answered, "but will he want the job?"

Ben and I met with Ed and several other GOP leaders three days before Thanksgiving. He wanted me in on the decision making. Kathy couldn't make the meeting, but I knew that the decision would eventually come from the two of them, after much prayer. Ben asked a lot of detailed questions about personal support and fundraising. I felt strongly that he could get a lot of financial support from car dealers around the state. He told them that he would give them his decision by the end of January. I felt that his chance of being elected was good. Kathy invited our family over for dinner on Thanksgiving Day....got a lot of input from Kathy and Amy. Kathy has always let Ben do what he wanted to do in matters like this but not before she had her say, giving him much to think about.

Amy's input was a simple statement. "Our country desperately needs the moral and conservative leadership right now that Ben can offer. I want him to run," looking at Kathy and holding her hand as she said it. Kathy's concern was about Ben living in Washington. She and the kids would miss him. Ben offered that Dannie was in Nashville, attending Vanderbilt, and came home from school only at the end of each semester. Sarah would be graduated from high school in six months and then she would be away at college, too, so the kids were not a factor in the decision.

He added that he would be home in Chattanooga much of the time out of necessity, meeting with constituents about particular problems, when Congress is not in session and when he was campaigning. "And if you're worried about the business, Tommie Crowell has already proved that he can manage the dealership quite well with a minimum of input from me," he explained. I injected that a decision didn't have to be made right away, so we all have plenty of time to think about it.

Ben and I watched the Cowboys and Redskins play football on TV. We listened to but didn't quite discern a lot of hushed conversation coming from the kitchen as Amy helped Kathy put away the dishes. Amy told me later that Kathy really wanted to hear what she had to say about Ben running for Congress...pleased Amy.

Nine

Our family spent five days in Gatlinburg over the New Year Holidays with Ben, Kathy and Sarah…tradition continues. Dannie couldn't make it. His Vandy basketball team was playing in a holiday tournament in Hawaii. Kathy told us that Ben would run for congress, they had decided. They would tell the local GOP next month but the public would not be informed for nearly a year, with the election being nearly two years away.

"We need to begin planning now, learning everything about the incumbent Democrat…what he professes to believe…his voting record…who his cohorts are…everything. We must be prepared if we're going to win," Ben said, sounding much like a football coach getting his team ready for the upcoming season.

1989 flew by us like a hurricane. Business was good for Ben. New car sales soared and he enjoyed record profits. Over the past eleven years Ben did a very smart thing because of his conservative nature. He plowed all of his profits into completing his buyout agreement and paying off the note to the bank for his dealership property and facilities. On January 1, 1990, Ben made his last payment to the bank for his land and buildings, retiring the loan three years ahead of time. He now owned his Ford franchise lock, stock and barrel…a good feeling. He felt more comfortable than ever about letting Tommy Crowell have control of the dealership. He was in full campaign mode, concentrating almost entirely on the congressional campaign that would end in ten months.

Ben formally announced that he would be seeking the Republican nomination for our congressional seat on the steps of the county courthouse. With a big American flag in the background, he stood in front of a few well wishers and every TV and radio station reporter in the area. Ben had not cut his own TV and radio spots for the dealership for five months. It's not allowed during the campaign, so we took him off the air early to avoid controversy. He and I decided that he would cut all of his campaign spots. Now when people saw him on TV or heard him on the radio it was Ben trying to sell them on his ideas of how government should be conducted, not why they should be buying a new Ford from him. We didn't refer to the Democrat incumbent during the Primary, just talked positively about Ben's philosophy of government and what he intended to do as our Representative. He won the Republican Primary in May by a landslide.

Now we had to prepare for the General election in November against an incumbent who had been there for eight years, with the full support of the Democrat Party. I knew of Ben's deep convictions about how our government should be run, having listened to him express them in our strategy meetings. I convinced Ben that we should use 60 second TV and radio spots rather than the 30 second spots we used in the Primary and which are normally used by other candidates. This would give him the opportunity to more thoroughly explain the details of his beliefs, rather than string together a few catchy sound bites that might leave the voter hanging. He liked the idea and added that each commercial should be issue oriented. We'll state the facts of the incumbent's voting record on each issue and we'll tell what Ben would do differently. Early polls had Ben behind by 6-7 points...much work to do.

The Chattanooga chapter of Christian Athletes in Action was holding what they called a "summer rally" in Chattanooga the last week in June. Over 600 high school and college aged young men and women of all races would be in attendance. Ben was asked to be one of the guest speakers back in March and he accepted. His opponent declined the invitation. He never was an athlete

: Ben would have an advantage in that ...um. The auditorium was filled to capacity, over 700 people with all of the reporters from newspapers, TV and radio stations and their crews. I was there, too, with a copy of the speech entitled "Faith and Patience" that I had helped Ben write, not that he would ever refer to it during his actual presentation.

Ben had a knack for getting the listener's attention and never letting it go during a speech. Here he was at his best and as usual he never looked down at his notes...engaged his audience...looked them in the eye as he walked the stage from left to right...came close to the front edge...leaned down at times so he was nearly up against the front row of seats. He knew what he wanted to say to these young people because they were just like him, *athletes* and *believers*. He told them of his faith in a way that true believers in Christ would understand. It is a faith that required patience to allow God to work in his life... in God's own time, not his.

He spoke of his father's example of faith and patience...enlisting in the Army during World War II after graduating from college on a football scholarship...of how God placed him in situations where he became one of World War II's most decorated heroes, rising in rank to First Sergeant of the all black infantry company in which he served. He told them of his dad's service in the Korean War five years later as a Company First Sergeant of the newly integrated U.S. Army...of how God again placed him in situations where heroic action was required, allowing him to rise to the rank of Brigade Sergeant Major, the highest rank that an enlisted man can obtain.

"Here's the important point," Ben said. "For six months in a hospital in Japan, as he lay recuperating from the wounds he suffered in a battle on a Korean hillside, he never once doubted that God was in control of everything...that all of this was in His will...and would be revealed to him someday as he patiently watched God at work... as events took place in his life over the next few years."

He went on to tell them that after his dad retired from the Army, he was offered jobs to coach and teach at the high school level. But as usual, he took a job in a place where "God wanted him to be," as a lowly laborer in the maintenance shop of the largest paper mill in the world. "As a boilermaker helper, everyone respected my dad. They knew he did an exceptional job helping each of the certified boilermakers that he was assigned to on a given day...never any trouble... always cooperative," Ben explained. "Sometimes he would come home to my mother tired, dirty, cuts and bruises from the physically demanding job. Mom would ask him why he didn't quit... teach and coach. He would remind her that they had prayed about it and knew that this is where God wanted him to be. Then one day, three years after he began work there in the shop, an experienced boilermaker was hired into the shop. He came from another paper mill. Things changed for my dad that day. This new hire was one of my dad's squad leaders in the Korean War. He told the shop foreman and over the next few weeks he told other workers in the shop how my dad saved his life and the lives of eight others in this man's rifle squad on a hill in Korea. Dad was wounded in the process and received a Purple Heart."

Ben went on to explain that about half of the men in that shop were veterans of World War II or the Korean War. Many were decorated combat heroes, too. "Strange thing about men who have served in combat…they don't like to talk about their experiences…no matter if they were combat heroes or just a soldier who did his job day in and day out. When they were told about my dad's heroism they knew he was one of them. He had never said a word about the two Purple Heart Medals he had received. These men of The Greatest Generation had a profound respect for my dad from that day forward."

"God was not through with my dad in the maintenance shop, the place where, he believed, God wanted him to be. No, His plan for my dad was not complete," Ben stated. He told of his dad's boss, the Maintenance Shop foreman, who was curious enough to check out his dad's war record. His boss had a brother who was a career officer stationed at the Pentagon. That officer discovered that his dad was nominated by his commanding officer to receive the Congressional Medal of Honor for his heroic action during World War II. Record keeping in battlefield conditions was difficult and, as it turned out the paperwork was never completed, forgotten as the war ended. His dad's commanding officer in Korea thought that his heroic action was deserving of the Medal of Honor there, too. Again, wartime record keeping didn't allow for the paperwork to be completed and processed up the chain of command.

"The Pentagon investigators concluded that my dad should be awarded a Medal of Honor for each action in the two wars, adding that only fifteen men in the history of The Congressional Medal of Honor, since the Civil War, have been awarded the medal twice. "This was not the first time that wartime record keeping denied heroes of medals that they rightly deserved. This happens often, so I don't want you to think that it was racially motivated. The Pentagon concluded that it was simply another case of sloppy wartime record keeping," he explained.

He went on to tell them of his dad being the first black man to become a certified boilermaker in the shop...being promoted to assistant foreman of the shop...then later becoming the foreman of the shop when his boss retired...easing the way for the entire plant to be desegregated in 1963...and, indeed, the entire city of Savannah.

"That was God's purpose for my dad. He was *ready* for God's call...he was *faithful* to His call...he was *patient* as God fulfilled His purpose through my dad." Ben continued by saying that God has a plan for each of them and that they should be ready for His call...trust Him with obedience....and patiently work as God unveils His plan through events that take place in their lives. More than fifty young people seventeen to twenty-three years of age, all races, approached us after his speech and offered to work as volunteers for Ben throughout the campaign. I took down their names and phone numbers as Ben talked to them.

Ben and I planned our traditional family vacation the first week in July, at a beachfront house in Panama City. This would give us a chance to relax a little before beginning the grueling campaign ahead of us. Dannie couldn't make it...attending summer school at Vanderbilt to make up for some classes he missed during basketball season. Anna and B.J. stayed with the adults most of the time, but Bennie fifteen, Sarah seventeen, and Neva thirteen were all "too big to be supervised so closely." We let them do as they wished and play on the beach by themselves, cross the highway and go to the amusement park by themselves and to go to a hamburger stand by themselves. Kathy and Amy were not too comfortable with the idea and reluctantly agreed to let it happen. The kids enjoyed their freedom...we did, too...gave us a chance to get a lot of talking done. Ben and I still got up before everyone else and greeted the sun as we ran along the white sands of Panama City beach and when sprint time came at the end of the run I knew that I could take him…I was always faster.

The news that Iraq had invaded Kuwait and taken over their oil fields was a shock to the whole world. It had a drastic effect on the car business. New car sales slowed down considerably. All of my dealers began cutting back their advertising budgets. Tommy did the same for Ben's dealership, ordering fewer vehicles and even laying off a few people to cut expenses. This one action by Saddam Hussein hurt the U.S. economy. Ben didn't let it bother him. He worked tirelessly on the election campaign, speaking to different groups and organizing his volunteers to canvass most of the neighborhoods and subdivisions door to door. Almost every evening between 4 pm and 8 pm, Ben personally went door to door in many neighborhoods in the Congressional District. I went with him on occasion and saw how effective he was in one-on-one situations with voters. I believe the impression that he made on them had a multiplier effect, motivating them to endorse Ben to other people.

There were two televised debates between Ben and the Democrat incumbent. Ben handily won both and pulled slightly ahead in the polls two weeks before the election. His conservative views rang true with voters…didn't matter if he was a black man…won the election by six points. The disappointment that Ben shared with me was that only 9 percent of black voters chose him… it hurt Ben…despite the fact that no Republican had ever received more than 5 percent of the black vote in East Tennessee.

Ten

Ben went to Washington and immediately set up his office, hiring only half the people that most Congressmen had on their staffs. He kept it lean and mean, as he always did. He had asked me to come with him, knowing the answer would be no. The young men and women on his staff were lawyers, economists and financial specialists, all with strong Christian conservative backgrounds. They were carefully chosen for their dedication and experience...and from the former Representatives and Senators they worked for. They would do the research Ben needed to make decisions on legislation that would come before him. He hit the ground running, immersing himself in pending legislation, Budget Committee assignments and getting to know the other Tennessee Congressmen and the congressional leaders of the Republican Party.

Ben didn't return home to Chattanooga during his first month in office. We talked over the phone a few times and not once did he speak of the dealership or Tommy Crowell. Ben had resigned from the dealership and Tommy was in full control of all operations. In just four months, Ben would sell his great Ford dealership to National Dealers, Inc, a big corporation that owned more than thirty new car franchises around the country. The seven million dollars netted from the sale would be placed in a required blind trust and administered by an investment firm, with no contact from Ben. At 48 years of age he committed himself to a new direction for his life…one of service to his country. "God had a plan for my Dad…has a plan for me…has a plan for America. I will involve myself in God's plan for the rest of my life as he reveals it to me," Ben told me over coffee one morning.

My life would take a change in direction, too, at 48 years of age. March 9, 1991, two days after my birthday, our Pastor asked me to consider becoming a Lay Speaker in the United Methodist Church. Lay Speakers are trained to preach and lead a worship service, through a series of weekend meetings led by local pastors. Lay Speakers, upon being "certified", would fill in for pastors of smaller Methodist churches as needs arise...sickness, vacations, etc. Amy and I talked and prayed about it for several weeks. I felt the call to do this, but what about the family? What toll would it take on them? After much prayer and consideration with Amy, and the children on occasion, the family encouraged me to pursue my calling to become a Lay Speaker. I had no idea where this would lead me at the time, but I had a peace and excitement about my decision.

I began speaking to small, rural United Methodist Churches in the valleys and on the mountains all around Chattanooga. Attendance would range from 30 to 125 at the various small churches which invited me to be their guest speaker while their pastor was away or sick. I rarely spoke to the same church twice, so I didn't have to prepare a lot of different sermons. After doing the same sermon three or four times, I had them practically memorized so I didn't need to refer to my notes often.

I began reading books about the history of Religion in America, a subject which captivated me for a few years. I was fascinated by the early settlers of our country and their dependence on faith in God to get them through the tough times. From the Pilgrims to those hearty souls who settled the West after the Civil War, faith in God was important to their ability to persevere under extremely difficult tasks. I am totally convinced that the Revolution could not have been won without a Godly man, George Washington, leading an army of Godly men. Nobody expected them to defeat the most powerful army in the world, but they did. There are so many eye witness accounts of miraculous events that took place in the battles of the Revolutionary War. You would have to conclude that God had a direct hand in producing the outcome, answering the prayers of Washington and many others.

Believing that, I became very concerned that today many people seemed to want to remove God from our public lives. They want to require Him to appear only at our churches and synagogues. I began to speak of those miraculous events which took place in the Revolutionary War in my sermons to the small rural churches that had asked me to fill in for their pastor on given Sundays. I tied together the history of our country with the faith in God that our founders shared openly and publicly. I refuted those who cry for the "separation of church and state" as their basis for removing God from public life. The "freedom of religion" clause in our Constitution simply states that (1. there will be no official government sponsored religion or church, as was the Church of England, and (2. that we are free to practice our choice of religion anywhere, not just in the confines of our church property or homes.

The concept of our freedom to practice our religion in public places began at the Constitutional Convention when Ben Franklin, seeing a tired group of delegates who were ready to give up and go home because no consensus had been reached, suggested that they go back into the meeting hall and "Pray to the God that saw them through the recent War." They did as he suggested and shortly produced one of the greatest documents ever written.

After these sermons on "God and Country" some members wanted to talk with me, asking questions about events and facts that I revealed. That rarely happened when the topic of my sermons was another subject. Sitting out in the pews, Amy recognized that these sermons about our history and faith were resonating with those around her, in every church I spoke to. By then I knew the subject so thoroughly, that I had it memorized. I knew exactly what I wanted to say. I usually walked around the pulpit area and got a little closer to the pews as I had seen Ben do, making it more dramatic. Seeing this, Amy suggested that a black, pin-striped suit wasn't effective for someone speaking of a time over 200 years ago. I needed a period costume. I laughed, and then I thought about it. That would certainly add to the drama and appear more realistic.

We ordered a costume complete with knee length pants and stockings, ruffled shirt, vest and coat. I even bought a pair of gold-framed eyeglasses. When I combed my hair straight back with no part Amy said that I looked a lot like Ben Franklin. This affect had a good outcome. I now spoke as a person from that century, telling them how it really was and what they should be looking out for in their time. I noticed that the people seemed to be paying closer attention as I spoke… gave me much more eye contact than before the costume. It was a good move and Amy was pleased that it was her idea. Soon I began to get requests from some of the larger churches to be a guest speaker at their worship services. Now the audiences numbered 200-600 people.

Ben and I talked at least once a week, now… sometimes two or three times. He trusted his best friend and sought my opinion on a variety of legislation that was being discussed before the House of Representatives. Plus, facing re-election every two years, we were always in campaign mode, so we had much to talk about concerning issues before congress and raising money to finance his re-election campaign. Ben said that he wanted to spend some time together next week when he came home for a long weekend. Kathy called a few days later and invited us over for Sunday dinner after church. It was a Sunday when I would be speaking to a local church at their morning service, so we invited them to attend with us. Both of our families were there.

Over dinner that afternoon, Ben couldn't help poking fun at my costume. "Amy was right, you do look like Ben Franklin….pot belly and all," he laughed. "But, the message was great," he added. Kathy said that I should speak to all of the high schools, adding to the secular history that they receive. Ben told us of a group of about 75 congressmen who meet weekly for breakfast, prayer and a short Bible reading. He thought that it would be a good idea for me to speak to his group since much of their discussions lately had centered on faith and morality in our country. Plus, it would give me more insight into the workings of our government and the problems Ben is facing.

Ben and I spent four hours that afternoon after dinner making plans for his first re-election campaign in the fall of 1992. He would have no challenge in the Republican Primary in May, so we concentrated on the General Election in November. We had plenty of money to spend thanks to the Republican Party and a group of auto dealers across the state who gave generously. Amy and Kathy had already planned a family vacation to Myrtle Beach in August. The four of us could write scripts for TV and radio commercials and Newspaper ads while we weren't on the beach or amusement parks with the kids. I would have all of the media buys in place by that time. As busy as this vacation was, Ben and I managed to get up each morning for a sunrise run on the beach, with our traditional sprint at the end… beat him every morning…never could outrun me.

Ben had become so popular and his job approval ratings were so high that no Democrat wanted to run against him in the general election. The candidate they chose was never in the race.

Ben got 62% of the vote. He still managed only 12% of the black vote, disappointing him greatly. The Democrat Party did a good job of painting Ben as an "Uncle Tom", doing his white master's will. They still didn't know who Ben was, owing himself to no man. He vowed to me that he would do a better job of positioning himself in the Black Community before the next election. Ben took his seat in the 103rd Congress, January 1993.

The year passed by quickly. The advertising agency was doing well even though I was spending less time with it. My lay speaking at area churches was taking up more time than ever. The guys were managing all of the accounts now, and all I did was to look in on their work often enough to make sure that it met my standards of what good advertising and marketing should do. Kathy set up my bookkeeping system with checks and balances so that with a quick look each month I could see how we stood financially.

Ben depended upon me more, too, continuing to trust me above everyone else to arrive at good decisions. I found myself traveling to Washington one week out of the month to help Ben on particular projects. On one such trip he asked me to bring along one of my Ben Franklin costumes and speak to his prayer breakfast group.

My presentation to the congressmen went well. Several of them stayed around afterwards for more discussion. A congressman from Texas said that every new immigrant into our country needs to hear this message. "They know that they are coming to a great country but they don't have a clear understanding of what has made us great...and with so many coming into the U.S. every day, I'm afraid that the roll our faith plays will be diluted over the years...causing us to lose our greatness."

A Representative from a mid-western state added, "I'm concerned about what I perceive to be our declining moral conscience as a nation." Then she said that perhaps I could make this presentation to the Congress as a whole...or even to a joint session of the House and Senate. I could tell by his "Big Ben Grin" that he was proud of his best friend's reception by his closest legislative allies. I was encouraged to know that so many of our lawmakers were devout Christians who recognized the importance of morality in a free society...and the necessity of religion for morality to prosper.

Dannie graduated from Vanderbilt in June with a 3.8 grade point average. He would attend Dental School at the Medical College of Tennessee in Memphis, wants to be an oral surgeon. Sarah finished her second year of college, majoring in Music and Theater at Middle Tennessee State University. Bennie completed his junior year in high school. All of the kids were doing well in their different schools, active in various sports and arts. Amy was promoted to a Major Accounts Manager at the newspaper, which meant that she, too, would have to travel out of town occasionally to make sales calls on Wal-Mart, Lowes, etc. Kathy was made a partner by her accounting firm and was appointed to the Board of Directors of one of our local banks. She now had fewer accounts to manage, so that was good from a time standpoint. Life was good for the West and Fleming households as 1993 came to an end.

Ben was appointed to serve on the House Appropriations Committee and The House Energy Committee, both of which he requested. The Appropriations Committee is the most powerful one in the House of Representatives. All spending bills must originate here, so this committee holds the "Power of the Purse". A Representative on this committee has a better chance of being re-elected each time because he has more opportunity to steer money his way…"bringing home the bacon." Ben discovered that lobbyists and special interest groups wanting money from Congress gladly give committee members campaign money, making it easier for them to get re-elected. Ben quickly learned how the game was being played…why government spending was always more than revenues received. Early on he concluded that there is no end to Congress's ability to spend money. And there is no end to requests for government money from lobbyists and self centered groups with the most frivolous projects…. projects that would benefit only those businesses and groups wanting the money.

Ben was convinced that budget deficits would continue to grow the debt as long as we had the ability to borrow money....as long as the fiscal attitude of Congress stayed the same. He began to speak out against some of these ridiculous bills introduced in the committee, appealing to the sanity of other members to reject this wasteful spending...voting against the bills. Some of his cohorts didn't appreciate his outspokenness and told Ben so. They voted against him on spending bills that he did support. Ben figured that he was making some enemies, but they would know that he was consistently true to his principles.

In March of 1994, Ben was home for a week. We began planning for his re-election campaign, knowing that he would have no opposition in the Primary because his approval ratings were so high. He wanted to campaign on the idea that he has not and will not accept money from lobbyists and, therefore, he will not "Bring home the bacon". He will not vote to provide funds that will satisfy particular groups of people and no one else. We knew that his liberal Democrat opponent, state senator Walt Hatcher, would argue that Ben was not getting enough money coming back into our Congressional District...that Ben was not getting the job done "for the people." Walt would play right into our hands, offering a very clear choice to voters. Ben would champion smaller government and lower taxes...his opponent, more spending and higher taxes.

His plan to win over the black vote was simple. He would speak to as many area churches, schools, colleges and civic groups as possible with his message that less government involvement in our lives means more independence, more opportunity and lower taxes. Kathy would be responsible for setting up those appearances. She began immediately, setting up meetings at churches all over the district, requiring Ben to be home almost every weekend. "It will take time and patience, so let's start now." she told Ben.

Two weeks later, Kathy had Ben speaking to the New Community Chapel, an independent inner city church with over 3,000 members. Ben would speak to both morning worship services…normally attended by 1,200 at each service. When she told Ben that it was a church that preached Black Liberation Theology she offered, "You might want to back out of the appearance."

Ben said, "No, this is just the audience I want." She advised him to be careful of the words he chose to say to them. He invited Amy and me to attend with him and Kathy.

The pastor introduced him from a brief script of Ben's bio…mostly college, brief professional football career, new car dealer and of his teaching his adult Sunday school class at his church.

Ben began as he usually did by telling the story of his Godly parents, both graduating from college and stressing education to him and his sisters…taking them to Jasper Springs Baptist

Church every Sunday…growing up in the housing projects of Savannah. "That's where I met my best friend when we were only a year old, and we've been best friends all of our lives." He asked me to stand up and introduced Amy and Kathy, also. I noticed some surprised looks when some of the congregation realized that I was white… including the pastor.

"I came to Dan's house every day with my Mom. She raised us from one through nine years of age while his mother worked as a welder in the shipyards of Savannah during the day. My mom read books to us every day as she put us down for our naps and eventually taught us to read before we entered school. Much of our time together was spent outside playing games with other kids in the neighborhood. We were inseparable and became best friends. Neither of us could understand that when it came time for the first grade I would go to an all black school and Dan would go to a white school."

He then told of our separation for eight years when my folks built a house in Garden City… how we cried that last day that we would have together…thinking that we would never see each other again. "It was at this time growing up in the fifties and sixties that I began to understand the 'Institutional Racism' we had to deal with. It was a racism that was focused not so much on one white person hating all black people. No, it was a system that had all white people living together in one neighborhood, sending their kids to an all white school, going to their jobs where fellow employees were all white, attending an all white church....and they don't see anything extraordinary about that."

Ben went on to say, "Thanks to Dr. Martin Luther King and many other civil rights leaders, including Presidents Eisenhower, Kennedy and Johnson, institutional racism of that degree does not exist today. Many of us now live in racially mixed neighborhoods all around Chattanooga. Big companies are actively recruiting us for jobs, employing us and promoting us to better paying jobs because we are capable and competitive. Most schools are integrated now. More of our kids are graduating from college and pursuing careers of all kinds. We are making more money, buying bigger houses and creating wealth that can be passed on to our children and grandchildren."

It was at this point in his sermon that he stepped down from the pulpit and walked out in front of the first row, without his notes to refer to. The pastor was still behind Ben in the pulpit area sitting in his chair. He flashed his "Big Ben Grin" and I knew that he would now begin speaking from his heart...as he got up close and personal with his audience...walking from side to side and establishing eye contact with them all.

"Yes, life is good for many of us, much better than it has been in the past. There is much to be done, however, so that living in America can be better for our children. Before welfare legislation was passed in the late sixties, our black family unit was strong. But look at what the Aid to Dependent Children Act of Congress did to us. It gave incentive to young women to have children without the thought of getting married first...and that has devastated our society."

Ben slowly walked to the left side of the church, surveying their faces. "Before this welfare act in the mid sixties, only 22% of black children were born out of wedlock. Today 73% are born out of wedlock...and that has destroyed traditional family life for us...so many homes without the guiding hand of a father. So, I'm not as much concerned about white racism. I'm more concerned about what we are doing to ourselves...the breakdown of our families. The family unit is not a creation of government or society. It is from God...right from the beginning...Adam and Eve. It's the cornerstone of our human existence. It must break God's heart to see what has happened to us. This is the truth that we must deal with. There's no denying the facts."

You could hear a pin drop on the carpet of the church as he faced them, walking from one side of the church to the other...all eyes on him. "I can look at you folks and guess that you might come from all types of family backgrounds. Some of you have plenty ...some just get by...some may be poor. You might be from a large family or a single parent. It doesn't matter where you came from, or where you are today. What is most important is where you are going....where will you be tomorrow? In this great country of ours there is no reason for you to stay where you are unless you want to stay. It's your choice. You have the greatest gift any government can give you...opportunity... there for the taking...no excuse for failure."

Ben walked back to the other side, studying them as he walked slowly. He could see on their faces what some were thinking. "If you think that all of the problems facing black Americans today are caused by white people...that's wrong. If you think that if you are ever going to prosper, it is someone else's responsibility, not your responsibility...then you will fail as an individual. You will never have that abundant life that Jesus promised." Everyone there knew that Ben had the track record to back up his words.

"You might have the mental attitude that there has always been white oppression and always will be...that's our life. That kind of thinking traps you into believing that you are a victim of white oppression...and that is simply not true. Seeing yourself as a victim helps you justify failure, 'blame it on the other guy.' That can lead to a lack of effort on your part, 'no sense in working hard, I'm never going make it.' Seeing yourself as a victim means you are willing to settle for less... even a meager government handout. You and your children deserve more."

Ben leaned in closer to the front row of pews and said, "I thank God that I live in a country where our capitalistic society is driven by our God given inner drive to compete…to be the best that we can be. Some of our nation's leaders want to move us to a socialistic democracy, knowing that socialism is equal to non-competition…everyone gets the same no matter how hard you work. That system of government has failed everywhere and every time it has been tried."

Ben then compared capitalism to two football players competing for the same position on a football team. "You know, I worked hard to develop my speed and abilities. I spent extra time in the weight room and ran extra wind sprints after practice. When others went home after a grueling practice and watched TV, I studied my play book. I knew all of my routes to run and the changes to make if the play broke down and the quarterback had to scramble. My hard work showed up in practice scrimmages. It helped me perform better than those competing for my position as a wide receiver. The coaches don't just say, then, that all receivers at my position will get equal playing time. No, they want to win so they play the one that's going to give the team the best chance of winning. That's what they get paid for, and they don't want to lose those high paying coaching jobs. If you watch much college and professional football, you can clearly see that those coaches don't care what color your skin is. They are going to play the best man."

He went on to say, "That's how our capitalist economy works, too. Business owners and managers want the best educated, best trained, highest performing people in every job at every level of operation...from entry level positions to upper level executives...and they don't care what color their skin is. They just want you to help them compete in the marketplace. Of course, racial prejudice still exists...we all know that. It's not so prevalent today, however. There are so many business owners and managers who are not. There are those in our society and government who will tell you that you can't make it on your own...don't believe them."

Ben stopped in the center and looked from side to side as he paused. "My personal experience tells me that this simply is not true. John Bannerman owned several new car dealerships in our state. He hired me as an entry level salesman at his new car dealership in Nashville. He promoted me to sales manager because I was a top salesman. Later he promoted me to General Manager of one of his other dealerships which was struggling, because I succeeded as a sales manager. That dealership grew and prospered under my management and he gave me the chance at owning a Ford Dealership in Chattanooga...buying it from him over a period of time. He was a white man who could have chosen anyone, but he picked me...because he knew that I would do the job successfully...didn't care about the color of my skin."

Ben paused and walked to the middle of the floor. "I know that conditions are far from being perfect. You 'will be denied opportunities' because pockets of racial prejudice still exist in our society," he said. "Experiencing that is no reason to give up. There is so much opportunity for you right now. I pray that you will see yourself not as a victim of society, but one who is in search of opportunity. God has a plan for each of us, and it is a plan for success, not failure. God doesn't want us to settle for less than what He has in store for us. It won't be easy for many of you. It's a longer, harder road, but taking that road is the only way to a better life for you and your family. The choice is always yours to make."

Ben repeated his message to the second service that morning, receiving a warm applause from each group. He gave the same presentation to as many churches as his schedule would allow during the campaign. We backed this up with similar commercials on the two urban radio stations and the results were good. Ben won the '94 election, getting 66% of the vote, including 22% of the black vote. He was happy but he still thought he could do better.

Ben also made speeches that Fall to support the Republican National Committee's "Contract with America," the Newt Gingrich-led effort to gain control of Congress from the Democrats. Ben spoke in nine different states on behalf of Republican candidates while promoting his party's "Contract with America." His message of less government spending, more personal responsibility, lower taxes and balancing the federal budget resonated with voters everywhere he went. The Republican Party gained a majority of seats in both the House and the Senate…first time in forty years. Ben's national popularity grew during this time and Republican groups of all kinds, all over America began asking him to speak at their gatherings.

This re-election campaign was a strenuous one. Ben and Kathy were very tired…so were Amy and I. We each decided to celebrate a quiet Christmas with our families and then flew everyone to the Bahamas for five days…our annual New Year celebration vacation together. Dannie and Bennie were pals, talking mostly about college experiences and their futures. They took B.J. along with them most of the time…snorkeling, jet skis, parasailing and other fun stuff on the beach. Sara, Neva and Anna split their time sunning on the beach, activities with the boys and occasionally shopping with Amy and Kathy. Ben and I spent much of our relax time sitting in beach chairs under a rented umbrella…reading, talking and sleeping. As usual we got up each morning before the sun came up to make our traditional sunrise runs on the beach…still sprinting the last hundred yards at 51 years of age…still faster than Ben.

As 1995 began with the 104th Congress in session, I found myself traveling to Washington more than ever. Ben really wanted me near because so much was happening…so fast. The Republicans were now in control of both Houses and Speaker Gingrich wasted no time in implementing the "Contract with America" that the Republicans promised. President Clinton vetoed the House Budget and because he and Gingrich couldn't reach an agreement, the U.S. Government was shut down in the fall of 1995. It was from this hard line stance on the budget, however, that Gingrich and the Congress achieved a balanced budget for four years…1996-99. The 104th Congress controlled spending like no other Congress in history. Ben and others on the Appropriations Committee cut spending…from Head Start to Environmental Protection…eliminating 320 Federal Programs altogether.

Two other laws that Ben and I worked hard on were passed. The Lobbyist Disclosure Act was a step in the right direction by requiring all lobbyists to register with the Congress. Ben hated this system of "lobbying for causes"…the root of all our spending problems. Despite the passage of this law, corruption and illegal practices could still occur. In August of '96, The Personal Responsibility and Work Opportunity Act (Welfare Reform) was passed. It requires welfare recipients to begin work after two years of receiving benefits. The law also strengthened the states' power to establish paternity and collect child support from fathers. The result is that by the year 2000, 53% of the welfare poor had been removed from the program.

It was the spring of 1996 and I was back in Chattanooga when Ben called. We talked for a few minutes about the upcoming primary and the general election that we had to prepare for in the fall. He mentioned the possibility of a challenge in the primary election, but didn't seem to be concerned because of his 64% approval rating. I could tell that something else was on his mind. He was concerned about a local project for which he had obtained funding from Congress in the amount of twenty-five million dollars. It called for harmful asbestos to be removed from four government housing projects in Chattanooga...an effort that was nationwide in its scope because of the health danger it presented. A non-profit group, the Community Action Housing Committee, applied for the funds to be used in tearing out and removing the old asbestos, remodeling the interiors of each apartment unit and installing all new appliances. The president of the CAHC was Robert Hart, a man who was experienced in acquiring Federal money for a variety of uses. He knew all of the procedures, and he was of some stature in the community. They would negotiate all construction contracts with local companies and suppliers, providing Congress with receipts and data backing up all transactions. "The project is only 30% complete and they have requested more than half of the money allocated for the job. I'm worried that there is too much waste. We need to check it out," Ben said. He was a firm believer that each Congressman should police his district's use of Federal funds to make sure that no waste or corruption was happening.

At Ben's direction, I took Kathy with me to inspect two of the job sites first, verifying the actual work being done as opposed to what the contract called for. We also counted inventory that was on site to do the job as opposed to what had been ordered and backordered and we checked time cards for each employee on the job. Kathy and I were on the first site at 7 am when everyone showed up for work. The site manager was surprised and somewhat nervous but he cooperated, knowing that we were from the Congressman's office. Kathy went right to work…knew what she was looking for…taking photos and counting inventory. I just walked around the place with the site manager as my guide, asking as many detailed questions as I could about the work going on and surveying work that was completed. I occupied as much of his time as possible. I didn't want him to call the office and warn them that we could come there next, giving them time to prepare for Kathy. I talked to several of the workers, getting as much information as I could.

At 10 am we drove to a second site and went through the same set of procedures. Kathy and I arrived at the CAHC office at 1pm. Robert Hart was there, along with his office manager and bookkeeper. Kathy tried not to arouse any suspicion but I could tell that everyone in the office was nervous. She got the bookkeeper to escort her around the office, sitting down with various clerks and questioning them about their jobs of handling specific records and receipts of the business that went on in the office. She examined a lot of the invoices, receipts and inventory listings…looking for the quality of materials specified and ordered as opposed to the quality of materials received and installed in each apartment. Periodically she would get up and walk over to the copier and make copies of some documents she had in her hand. I knew Kathy and by 4 pm I could see that her keen auditing eyes were astonished at the details she was uncovering. She got up from the last clerk's desk and motioned to me that she was finished. We thanked everyone for their cooperation and headed for the parking lot.

Before we had our seat belts buckled she blurted out, "Dan, this Hart is a crook. His hand is in every detail of this construction. What I see so far is that Hart is specifying, ordering and paying for building materials and appliances of a high quality. He is receiving and installing materials and appliances of lesser quality…at much lower prices. Also, it looks as though they have employees receiving paychecks who have never worked on the job and whom nobody knows. I'm guessing that they have bilked Congress hundreds of thousands of dollars thus far into the contract. Ben will want to stop it now and conduct a full audit before continuing."

Ben did just that, hiring a local accounting firm to begin immediately. It was not Kathy's accounting firm, but one of her competitors. He didn't want to have conflict of interest charges brought up in the trial that was sure to ensue. The audit didn't take long. Out of the 25 million dollar grant, Hart and his cohorts in crime had plans to siphon off more than 4 million dollars. Hart admitted his wrongdoing in a plea bargain deal that got him a reduced sentence. The local appliance dealer who was in on the scheme and the building materials dealer who faked invoices admitted to their roles in the fraud. They, too, received lesser sentences for their cooperation, saving taxpayers the costs of a trial. All of the money was recovered. Perhaps six to eight years in jail will cause them to rethink their actions.

The following week Ben was given time to speak to the House of Representatives from the floor of the chamber. He recounted details of the investigation, mentioning Kathy and me. "I have put everyone on notice in my district…no Congressional funds without my personal oversight. They must know that if they get money from the taxpayers it must be spent well. We owe them that much." He went on to encourage other Congressmen to do the same, saying that in the end it is "our responsibility to see that we don't misspend the taxpayer's hard earned money." He received a light round of applause from some who agreed with him, but most, Democrats and Republicans, seemed to have other things on their mind…not listening.

Every politician and his staff members keep talking about fraud and waste in government spending, but there doesn't seem to be a genuine effort to eliminate it. Furthermore, it bothered Ben that many of his conservative Republican friends in the House and Senate voted for some of the most frivolous spending bills right along with the liberal Democrats. Even though Congress would balance the federal budget for the next four years, he could still see billions of dollars of unnecessary spending…wasting taxpayer money…and few of them seemed to care.

Eleven

Dannie graduated from Dental School that summer of 1996. He went to work with a dentist in Nashville who planned to retire in six years, and entered into a buyout agreement with Dannie. He was excited about his opportunity. Kathy and Ben were glad that he was so close to home. Sarah received her degree in music and theater at the same time and was teaching at a local high school in Chattanooga. Bennie was in his final year at the University of Tennessee, majoring in architecture. Neva, in her second year at UT, was planning to be a teacher. Anna and B.J., still in high school, were doing well...makes me happy.

Ben again had no opposition in the primary. But this time he had a serious challenger in the general election in the Fall of 1996. Backed by the Democrat Party, Big Bill Colton, a state senator, was a formidable challenger at 42 years of age. His grandfather and his dad had become quite wealthy in the coal business from 1912 through the 1960's when coal was used to fire up most of the boilers in homes, office buildings and factories requiring steam to heat and power their facilities. When they converted to clean burning gas away from coal, the Colton's merely put their money in real estate, ending up with large holdings in land and office buildings today. Big Bill was 6 feet 5 inches tall and weighed 240 pounds...dark wavy hair and blue eyes...big handsome smile...friendly personality...always seemed to be winking at you...ready to talk about anything. The Democrats were excited about their candidate, thinking that he had a real chance to win, so they raised a lot of money for the campaign. Big Bill let it be known that he was willing to spend as much of his personal money as was needed to win. He would campaign hard. This election would be difficult for Ben.

The biggest thing going for Ben was his 98% voting record on conservative principles and his District approval rating of 65%. One other thing that lifted our confidence was that the local news media had done a good job of reporting on Ben's effort in Congress to help achieve a balanced federal budget for fiscal year 1996. Big Bill wanted three televised debates in October. Ben told me he would do two. At my urging, Ben settled for one debate, twelve days before the election... one day before early voting began.

Colton's campaigners began flooding the TV and radio stations with negative ads against Ben two weeks before I was to begin our media buy, catching us by surprise. Their ads featured several "no" votes Ben had made on spending legislation that would have sent money into the Tennessee Valley for things such as making repairs on dams and locks on the rivers and lakes. The ads failed to mention the millions of "pork" dollars that were attached to the legislation, the reasons Ben could not vote "yes" on those bills. We stuck to our guns and merely told of Ben's efforts to lower taxes and hold down government spending. The barrage of negative ads achieved the results they wanted. Big Bill closed the gap somewhat, the polls now showing Ben's lead narrowing to 53% of the vote to Colton's 45%.

In the televised debate the immediate contrasts were evident, Ben black, Big Bill white and Ben 5 feet 8 inches, Colton 6 feet 5 inches. I couldn't help but notice how Big Bill bent over at the waist ever so slightly as they shook hands to begin the debate. Was he trying to intimidate Ben right from the start? I knew that would not work on Ben. Colton was the aggressor throughout the two hour debate, constantly interrupting Ben before his time was up despite warnings by the moderator. Not once did Ben interrupt Colton while he was speaking. Ben answered each question from the moderator. Colton avoided many questions from the moderator and continued to go back and hammer Ben about his voting record that was not bringing federal money back into the district.

Big Bill really concentrated on Ben's support of Welfare Reform, claiming that it hurt many of Chattanooga's poor…saying Ben didn't care. Ben merely restated his position that after thirty years and billions of dollars poured into LBJ"S War Against Poverty, there is more poverty than ever. Nothing has been accomplished by all of that money except to pile up our country's debt. Most analysts agreed that Ben won the debate on both style and substance. Big Bill's aggressive stance paid off, however, as the polls taken four days after the debate narrowed again to 51% to 47%. The heaviest part of our media buy would take place from then until the day of the election. Ben and I both felt that we could hold our own until then, staying with the positive message of his efforts to lead our country to one of lower taxes and lower federal spending. Ben won re-election by 52% to 48%...a very satisfying win.

Amy invited Ben and Kathy over for Thanksgiving dinner, but they had to decline this year. His older sister in Savannah was hosting Thanksgiving dinner for their whole family. His dad's health had not improved since a recent mild heart attack so Ben was anxious to see John and Rebecca….hadn't seen them in nearly a year.

John West died on Friday after Thanksgiving with all of his family around him. He was 83. Kathy called and told us of the funeral that would take place on the following Monday.

Amy and I drove down to Savannah and visited my sister the day before the funeral. It was a military funeral of the highest honor. Hundreds of people were in attendance...political dignitaries from local, state and national governments... soldiers from nearby Ft. Stewart... men from the Maintenance Shop at National Paper...church members, neighbors and friends. There wasn't a dry eye in the place when John's close friend and pastor for the past twenty years delivered the eulogy. My dad always told me that size is not the measure of the man. I knew...I knew that John West was a giant of a man.

I spent time with Rebecca after the funeral talking about growing up during those early years of childhood with Ben. Looking back on those years, I can more clearly see all of the little things she taught us that shaped our character...made us better men. We hugged and said our goodbyes. Amy and I drove back to Chattanooga that night, getting home at midnight.

We didn't do the New Year Holidays with Ben and Kathy this year. They went to Savannah a week before Christmas and didn't return to Chattanooga until January 3rd, 1997. They needed to take care of the many family details that would finalize John's death. We rented a chalet high up in the Smoky Mountains near the ski lodge in Gatlinburg between Christmas and New Years day…just the six of us. Bennie left us two days early. It seems that he had to get back to Knoxville to a New Years Eve Party that a special young lady was having at her parent's house. Amy reminded me again that our kids were growing up, that we would soon be "empty nesters" like Ben and Kathy.

Ben was back in Washington on January 5th, 1997 to take his seat in the 105th Congress. That year he would join with his Republican colleagues to pass the Balanced Budget Act, calling for 160 billion dollars in spending cuts to reach a balanced budget by 2002. They also passed the Taxpayer Relief Act, reducing the top bracket of capital gains taxes from 28% to 20% and the 15% bracket to 10%. The 600 thousand dollar estate tax exemption was raised to one million dollars.

Anna was graduated from high school in June…starts nursing school in the fall. Bennie got his degree in architecture and was employed by a major construction company in Raleigh, North Carolina. B. J. would begin his senior year in high school this fall. The nest is emptying out.

I began spending more time in Washington than in Chattanooga now. Ben wanted so much from me that he put me on his Congressional payroll, making me his chief of staff. It was exciting work for me, felt like I was working for a greater good. Amy could sense that I was happy with the work that I was doing for Ben. She never complained that I was away so much of the time. We talked almost every night…missed her.

Ben had very little competition in his 1998 re-election campaign. He was assigned to the House Banking and Finance Committee in addition to his spot on the Appropriations Committee in the 106th Congress, 1999 and 2000. Ben now had the positions he wanted on the two House committees that had oversight for both the fiscal and monetary policy decisions for the United States government.

I began researching the work of the Banking Committee, giving my reports to Ben on a weekly basis. He wanted me to be with him at all committee meetings… giving me that look when he wanted me to pay close attention to the immediate subject of discussion and make detailed notes…so nothing is forgotten. We would discuss these issues thoroughly back in his office.

President's Clinton's impeachment took much time away from the legislative activity going on in the House. It did manage to pass another "omnibus" spending bill, full of the "earmark pork" that Ben hated. He fought hard against the bill but it passed with the votes of many of his Republican friends. "We keep spending more and more and the debt is piling up, now over five trillion dollars. When is Congress going to come to its senses?" Ben sighed in exasperation. One thing was certain to me, Ben's calling was clearly defined now…get spending under control and retire the nation's debt or we will fail as a free country…with a democratic republic and capitalism at the heart of our freedoms.

"America will not become another nation on the historical ash heap of those countries which failed to see what was happening to them as they made choices that were destructive to their future…not while I have a breath in my body," he told me. "You and I know what this country can do for anybody who has the desire to become better…to succeed if they are willing to prepare for it…to work hard for it. You and I must do all that we can to see that it is not only preserved for our children and grandchildren, but is made even better." Ben and I shared that calling together.

My lay speaking took another direction now that I'm spending so much time in Washington. Instead of speaking to churches around Chattanooga, I now began to speak at larger churches all over the country…mostly at the invitation of Congressmen who had heard me speak and who got to know me. My message was nearly the same at every church, "Let us hold on to the wisdom of presidents Washington and Adams who urged us to maintain a moral society because our system of government depends upon moral citizens…to vote for moral leaders to run our government…and religion is necessary to achieve morality. That's why we are encouraged by our Constitution to practice the religion of our choice everyday...everywhere."

The 2000 campaign for re-election was easy for Ben, won by 20 points. Not so for newly elected President Bush and Vice President Cheney. The Congress was split now, with a Republican House and a Democrat Senate, making it more difficult to cut spending and reduce our debt. During the fall campaign Ben spoke in support of his Republican allies in Congress at their election rallies and Republican Party fundraisers all over the country. He was a popular speaker in the party...everywhere he went...hammering home again and again his ideas of how we can regain fiscal and monetary sanity within our government to understanding listeners in every state in which he spoke. Ben was gaining in national prominence.

For most of 2001 we both traveled around the country, speaking to civic clubs, chambers of commerce, commencements, churches and, of course, the never ending political fundraisers of the Republican Party. My message to churches who asked me to speak was becoming more political in nature. My fear is that the mass immigration to the U.S. over the past two decades will dilute our wonderful heritage of government and religious beliefs that has made us strong. We must do a better job of educating each new generation of Americans of this great history of our founding and growth as a nation of God. We must, also, make certain that newcomers to our country have a clear understanding of why America is great. They want to live here because they know it will be good for them and their families. We must tell them why it is good.

One week each month Amy and Kathy would fly up to Washington to be with us. Ben and I made sure that we kept those planned weeks free from speaking trips. They enjoyed attending committee meetings with us and always came up with good suggestions for plans that we were working on.

On one such week, over dinner one evening, Kathy said, "Amy and I were talking in the plane on the way up here and were reminded that our families have been three years without our traditional summer vacation together."

"It has to be a pretty big place," I chimed in, "because we've added six grandchildren into the mix."

Amy added, "Kathy and I thought that a perfect place would be that big house we rented on Myrtle Beach when the kids were in their teens."

The big house on the beach was available, so we rented it for twelve days in July and invited all of the kids. Everyone made it except B.J. who was attending summer classes at the University of Tennessee. He had four days between sessions, so he drove over from Knoxville for a long weekend with the family before heading back to classes. Kathy met B.J. on the weathered wood front deck as B.J. arrived. She hugged him and said, "Now the whole family is here."

As we sat in our beach chairs under an umbrella, watching our children digging in the sand with our grandchildren, Ben remarked, "You know, Kathy is right. We are a family. Have you noticed how genuinely happy they are around each other…like brothers and sisters who haven't seen each other for a while."

"Yes, I have and so has Amy," I replied. "It looks as though this family tradition of vacationing together will continue long after you and I have left this world."

Ben and I didn't talk about things of Washington on this vacation…just spent time with the children, catching up on things…loving on the grandchildren…letting them get to know us better…spoiling them as only grandparents can do. Kathy and Amy seemed to be closer than ever…best friends. I believe the girls learned much from their mothers over the twelve days together…seemed to draw closer together, too. As usual, Ben and I got up before everyone else, greeted the sunrise on the sand and ran for two miles on the beach, sprinting the final hundred yards with me out front…was always faster than Ben. It was a fun and relaxing vacation. We went back to Washington ready for work.

Then, on September 11th, 2001 our world changed. One of the things we Americans love most is to wake up in the morning, have our coffee and go to our jobs...with no thought that somebody wants to kill us...no fear that anything bad could happen to us as we make our way to work. We Americans, enjoying security of our free society, are easy, unsuspecting targets for hate filled cowards who want to take advantage of us. Nearly three thousand New Yorkers left their families and loved ones that morning and said, "Be home for dinner tonight,"..."Be back in town in four days...I'll call each night from the hotel,"... "Want me to pick up the kids at the ball fields this afternoon?".... "Sure, I can stop and get some cereal and milk on the way home."

They were secure in the freedom that they had taken for granted all of these years... never thinking that they wouldn't see their families again. This precious gift of freedom was shaken on that day but it was not taken from us. No, they can never take that away from us. Our freedom is a gift from God...preserved by our forefathers... engrained in our hearts and minds...never to be relinquished to anyone.

Watching New Yorkers endure, survive, struggle, comfort and help each other in the days and weeks following 9-11 encouraged us all. As I watched President Bush standing in the rubble of the two fallen buildings with the bull horn in his hand, I was reminded of President Kennedy's speech in Berlin and thought, "I am a New Yorker!" My heart went out to them. We all became New Yorkers as we resolved with them to never let this cowardly group destroy our will for freedom...that along with Mayor Giuliani, we will continue to get up each morning and go to work...they won't stop us.

In the months following 9-11, I watched President Bush making timely and right decisions to track down the radical Islamists who were responsible. His tax cuts added 87 billion dollars of tax revenue to the Treasury, at a time when we would need the money to fight this new kind of war against Islamist Terrorism. It astonishes me when liberal Democrats complain every time responsible federal tax cuts are implemented, and it results in increased revenue to our government coffers. It happened when President Kennedy cut tax rates and when President Reagan cut tax rates.

I couldn't help but think "What would Al Gore do if he had won the election?" All of us in Tennessee know Gore and what he would do. The first thing he would do is raise taxes, like any good Democrat needing money. And, as in the first time the Islamist Terrorists attempted to blow up the Twin Towers, he would do as President Clinton did...nothing. He would not see it as a large group of well organized Islamist Terrorists waging war against us. He would treat it as a criminal action and lead us on a course that would invite our enemies to attack us again. His liberal mind wouldn't let him think that there actually was a large number of people who wanted to kill us...destroy our way of thinking...our society and culture...our religion. A President Al Gore wouldn't take this threat seriously, leaving us vulnerable to further very costly attacks on our people. Gore's policies would lead to a tax and spend government that would put our economy into a deep downward spiral that would take years to recover from. Yes, I know what Gore would have done, and I thank God that he was not our President.

Ben was easily re-elected to Congress in the Fall of 2002. Other Republican candidates continued to ask him to visit their Congressional Districts all over the U.S. to help them campaign, especially if they happened to be in a close race. Ben didn't need to campaign hard in our district, so he was available to attend rallies for fellow Republicans right up to the November elections. His national prominence grew and the TV and radio news and talk shows sought him out often. His message of morality and conservatism in our government livened up every interview he did... and his popularity grew each week.

The Republicans were back in control of the House and the Senate in the 108th Congress. In March, 2003 the U.S. invaded Iraq, suspecting that Saddam Hussein had weapons of mass destruction. He had already proved to everyone that he would use them. Much of our work during the next two years had to do with the war on terrorism. Ben and a few other House members did manage to get the Ban on Partial Birth Abortion Act passed through the House and the Senate.

On November 2, 2004, Kathy called Ben and told him that his mother had died suddenly of heart failure. I was in his office at the time of the call. We cried together. Rebecca was 85 years old. The funeral was a wonderful celebration of her life. The pastor didn't deliver a eulogy. Instead three of her closest friends, all teachers, spoke of her caring love that she freely gave to everyone...students, teachers, principles, church members and neighbors. The choir that Rebecca sang in for over thirty years sang "Beulah Land" and "The Old Rugged Cross," her favorites. Lots of tissues were used that day...wish Mom could have been there.

Republicans still had control of both Houses of Congress as the 109th Congress began in January, 2005. The wars in Afghanistan and Iraq were proving to be more costly than we thought and Congress was showing no desire to cut the budget in other areas, requiring more deficit spending. The result was that our accumulated debt grew to 7 trillion dollars by year end....never thought that it would ever get this high.

A number of Senators, including Senator Obama, initiated the Federal Funding Accountability and Transparency Act, requiring full disclosure of all businesses and organizations receiving federal funds. Ben and a few other Congressmen guided the bill through the House for passage. President Bush signed the bill making it law. It's amusing that the Democrats were all in favor of such a law when both houses of Congress and the President were Republicans.

Ben's popularity surged during this time, despite constant attacks from Democrats at home and liberal media on a national basis. He had become the most popular speaker on the conservative circuit. Radio talk shows asked him to be on their programs often and morning TV shows requested him every time he was available. During the fall of 2006 he had no challenge for reelection, so he was busy around the country speaking on behalf of his beleaguered Republican Congressmen and Senators.

The Democrats campaigned well, targeting vulnerable Congressional districts and key Senate races and getting their voters to the polls. They regained control of both houses of Congress and Nancy Pelosi became the first female Speaker of the House. Ben was worried now, knowing how the Democrats like to spend money on social programs. Our accumulated debt had reached the staggering sum of 8.5 trillion dollars, a figure that no one thought was possible five years ago. President Bush was handcuffed. If he wanted to continue funding the war on terrorism, he would have to compromise with the Democrats and that meant more spending on their social programs, more deficit spending and more debt added on to bring the total to 9 trillion dollars at the end of fiscal 2007.

The economy began sliding into a recession toward the end of 2007. At our first meeting of the Monetary Policy Oversight Committee with Federal Reserve Chairman, Ben Bernanke, in February, 2008 there was much discussion about what to do to stimulate the economy. Chairman Bernanke suggested a tax rebate to low and mid income people, plus shoring up Fannie Mae and Freddie Mac to back up the mortgages they were holding on all of those subprime loans made to people all over the U.S. These were loans made to individuals who couldn't afford to make their monthly payments. Introduced in the House and passed by the Democrats, the 152 billion dollar stimulus package was supposed to be enough to kick start the economy and provide enough money to keep Fannie, Freddie and the lending banks solvent. Ben and a number of other Republicans on the committee argued against more deficit spending, on top of the already monstrous debt, as a means to improve the economy.

As 2008 wore on, even larger numbers of those new home owners with subprime loans began defaulting on those loans. These borrowers with risky credit simply did not have the income to make the payments and cover the rest of the living expenses for their families. Lending banks had no choice but to foreclose on those loans and get Fannie and Freddie to cover their losses. This is another case where liberals, intending to "do a good thing for the poor," have created a disaster. As the lending banks looked to Freddie and Fannie for the funds to cover these bad risk losses, Fannie and Freddie ran out of money. In July Congress passed the Housing and Economic Recovery Act, giving an additional 300 billion dollars to Freddie Mac and Fannie Mae, funds needed to prevent a large number of bank failures, including some on Wall Street.

Not much was said about this looming financial catastrophe from Senator John McCain and Senator Barack Obama as they campaigned for the presidency that fall. Then America's housing mortgage crisis took full affect, causing financial panic here and around the world. Congressional leaders, President Bush and Treasury Secretary Paulson hurriedly passed the Emergency Economic Stabilization Act. It provided 800 billion dollars to be used to purchase the mortgage backed securities from U.S. and foreign banks, keeping them solvent. Once again, the American taxpayer, through the Federal Reserve, is called on to finance the Wall Street banks and the world's economy.

Ben's opposition to the bill in the house debate showed his fury over the injustice of the bill and its basic flaws. "We can't continue to put the burden on our fellow citizens to come to the rescue of banks who have taken unnecessarily high risks with the money in their vaults. These banks should be allowed to fail, go through a structured bankruptcy and recover, or they should be taken over by stronger banks. It is immoral to take money from the American taxpayer and give it to poorly managed banks acting out of greed."

This goes for the auto industry, too, of which Ben was very familiar. "Bailing them out and, thereby, letting them go through a government-structured bankruptcy is the wrong thing to do. It will keep in place the same old financial management practices that have caused them financial difficulty in the past, mainly leaving all of the labor union contracts and costly pension plans in operation. This assures that GM and Chrysler will be faced with the same financial problems at some time in the future. The only result of this action by Congress and the Federal Reserve for our country's citizens is to raise our accumulated debt even higher, a debt that our children and grandchildren will find impossible to pay."

President Obama was sworn in as President in January, 2009. Our government has added another trillion dollars to our accumulated debt, now totaling 10 trillion dollars. President Obama, the Democrat Congress and the Federal Reserve show no willingness to slow down spending and by the end of this year our debt as a nation will reach nearly 12 trillion dollars. Our interest payments on this debt now cost taxpayers over 200 billion dollars each year...insanity. At this point I began to see a change in Ben. He was angry at this situation and resolved to do something about it, but not knowing what to do at this point.

With a Democrat controlled House and Senate, early in 2010 President Obama crammed his Affordable Health Care Law down the throats of American taxpayers, 65% of whom did not want it. Few people really understood all of the provisions of "Obama Care," its' costs, its' impact on the medical profession and what it would do to small business owners and the jobs they provide. The part that scares me most is the hiring of an additional 16,000 IRS agents who would administer the plan, controlling 15% of our economy. The public was furious at the Democrat's disregard of the majority of Americans' views on government health care.

Our children were all grown and gone with families of their own now, fourteen grandchildren between the two families. Amy found a three-story house on the beach at Panama City that would sleep the twenty-four of us, first week in June. Sitting next to me under a big beach umbrella, Ben folded up the book he was reading, pointed to our children playing on the beach and in the water. "Look at them, Dan...doesn't that remind you of us on this same beach thirty-five years ago?"

"Yeaaah," I responded, "a good reminder. It makes me happy that they have always enjoyed this time together as a family. Like you, I can't help but wonder what their future will look like in thirty-five years."

At sixty-seven years of age, Ben and I still got up every morning before the sun for our traditional run on the beach...more like a slow jog now. Neither one of us broke into a sprint for the last hundred yards this time...no need to prove the point...was always faster than Ben.

Amy and Kathy had continued to come up to Washington each month. Those one week trips were stretching into two weeks and longer now that both of them had retired from their jobs. They loved getting involved in issues that Ben and I took on, helping us research and formulate opinions, something they are both good at doing. We lived next door to each other in adjoining townhouses in Alexandria...close to the capital.

Sarah's family, husband and three kids, at Kathy's insistence, have been living with Kathy in their big house in Chattanooga for the past two years. Neva and her husband were divorced last year, so she and her two children moved into our house with Amy. With our homes being occupied and cared for, Amy and Kathy were prepared to move to Washington full time to be with Ben and me. They especially like attending our meetings with the Federal Reserve System.

After one such meeting, we discussed the happenings over dinner. "Most Congressmen seem to be in awe of the Federal Reserve and I don't know why," Kathy said. "They certainly are not the experts on the economy that they are touted to be, what with all of the ups and downs our economy has endured over the many years that the FED has been in charge."

Amy added, "Some members of the Finance Committee are critical of the FED, asking a lot of questions that don't get answered and asking for written information that they never get and don't follow up on. It seems as though they are afraid to push the FED too hard for those answers."

Kathy responded, "I don't know of any major corporation that would allow one of its groups with this kind of power to operate so secretly independent...doesn't make good business sense. I don't like all of these secret dealings the Federal Reserve does with the Central Banks of other countries, transferring U.S. dollars to foreign banks in huge quantities, with no accountability. What I really can't understand is why both the Senate and the House lets them get away with it."

Ben looked at me. "Dan, do you ever wonder why so many newly elected Congressmen arrive in Washington with the idea that they and other newly elected Congressmen will change things, yet nothing ever gets done that is meaningful to make things better. It's they who change, becoming like every other lawmaker in Washington... yielding to the powers that be. And just who are these powerful people behind the scenes, this invisible government that pulls the strings on all of us?" Ben slowly rotated his head, looking at each of us and said, "I think Congress absolutely needs to audit the FED, but first, let's do some investigating of our own. Kathy, will you and Amy visit the Library of Congress and look back as far as you can on the history of the FED and all of their dealings and activities that could have affected our economy?" They quickly agreed.

Twelve

For the next two months, Kathy and Amy poured over Congressional records, read books of reference and met with Congressmen and Senators on the Banking and Finance Committees. They talked to career professionals at the U.S. Treasury Department, some of whom had retired from service, and interviewed economics and banking professors at major universities. What they had to tell us about the Federal Reserve was astonishing. Amy began, "This is going to take a while, so Dan why don't you get each of us a coke to go along with this popcorn that I've made." I returned with the cold drinks and she continued. "Most Americans think that the Federal Reserve System is part of our Federal government...not so. It is a privately owned banking cartel. Over 60% of the FED's stockholders are Europeans, owners of the world's biggest banks...in England, France, Italy and Germany primarily. American bankers who own a minority interest in the FED are the J.P. Morgan family, Lehman Brothers and the Rockefellers."

Amy went on, "One wealthy family owns controlling interest in all of these European Banks and, thereby, our Federal Reserve System...the Rothschilds. They began as money lenders in 1750 Germany, and spread their offices to Frankfort, Paris, London, Vienna, Brussels and Rome...becoming enormously wealthy in a few short years... controlling the issuance of credit and currency all across the European continent. Through payoffs and bribery they soon controlled the politicians of each country, establishing themselves as The Central Bank in all of these countries. They dictated the monetary policy of each country. With this power to issue currency, to lend money and control interest rates, the Rothschilds accumulated enormous wealth and power."

Amy stopped and took a sip of her coke. "The Rothschilds are a greedy bunch...wanted more. Being bankers, they made money by lending money...at reasonable interest rates...they set the rates. They discovered early on that wars between countries needing huge amounts of cash to finance those wars were very profitable...and a good bet to pay off their debts win or lose. During the Napoleonic Wars, the Rothschilds of France financed Napoleon and their Bank of England financed the British war effort...didn't matter who won, the Rothschilds made another fortune...and they were not above starting conflicts for profit, either. They mastered the art of staying quietly in the background, letting their paid-for politicians do their evil deeds."

Amy continued, "When America won its independence from England, the Rothschilds convinced Congress that they had the expertise to kick start this fledgling economy. In 1791 Congress gave the Rothschilds control of the U.S economy with a 20-year charter for a central bank, the First Bank of the U.S...to issue currency, to loan money and to set interest rates. Congress was not happy with their performance, so their charter was not renewed in 1811. Behind the scenes they got the British government to declare war on the U.S. as punishment. Under General Andrew Jackson, the British were defeated at New Orleans and driven back across the sea in 1814. In 1816, the Rothschilds bribed enough Congressmen with money from their private bank in New York to pass a law permitting another 20-year charter for a Rothschild central bank, the 2nd Bank of the U.S."

Amy took another sip from her coke and said, "Again, Congress and the people were not happy with the way the Rothschilds ran the economy and were bitterly opposed to a European- owned central bank of the U.S. In 1832 Andrew Jackson won the Presidency by campaigning on the promise that he will take control of the U.S. economy by abolishing the Rothschild's central bank. Jackson began immediately to remove government deposits and other assets from Rothschild banks and deposited them in U.S. Banks. The Rothschilds retaliated by contracting the money supply and calling in loans…causing a deep recession in the economy…blamed President Jackson. In 1835 an assassin tried to shoot Jackson at point blank range with two flint lock pistols, but both pistols misfired. The assassin, Richard Lawrence, claimed the he was hired by some wealthy Europeans. Jackson and his friends always believed it was the Rothschilds who tried to kill him…couldn't prove it."

Ben and I gasped. "There's more," Amy said, "During the Civil War, Abraham Lincoln went around to all of the large banks in New York to borrow money for the war effort. The banks were controlled by the Rothschilds. When they wanted to charge the government 24% interest on the loans, Lincoln was furious…printed up his own money to fund the war…450 million by the war's end. The people now had their own 'debt free and interest free' money…legal tender for the U.S. The Rothschilds hated Lincoln…Honest Abe couldn't be bribed. And they knew that a free U.S. economy, with its Christian work ethic, and opportunity-seeking citizens and immigrants would thrive in a system where it issued its own currency… debt free and backed by the full faith and trust of the U.S. government. The Rothschilds couldn't let that happen. They must have control over this ever-expanding U.S. economy... profitable for them. You see, what they really want is control of the world's economy and controlling America's economy is the key to that."

Amy put her drink on the table. "Addressing Congress in 1865 Lincoln said. 'I have two great enemies...the Southern army in front of me and the banks to my rear. Of the two, the banks are my biggest enemy.' Two months after he made this statement he was assassinated. Many of the President's closest friends in Congress, familiar with the Rothschild's tactics, believe they hired John Wilkes Booth to kill Lincoln....no proof though. Booth was killed ten days later before anyone could question him. Between the Civil War and the turn of the century the U.S. economy grew rapidly as we stretched our boundaries westward."

"The Rothschilds don't give up," Amy continued, "In 1881 they pushed hard on President James A Garfield, but he wanted nothing to do with a Rothschild central bank operating in the U.S. again. President Garfield was quoted in a speech to Congress, 'Whoever controls the volume of money in our country is absolute master of industry and commerce... and when you realize that the entire system can be easily controlled by a few powerful men at the top, you will not have to be told how periods of inflation and depression originate.' Two weeks later President Garfield, a very vocal Rothschild opponent, was assassinated."

Amy continued, "Still not giving up their quest of ruling the world, the Rothschilds increased their bank holdings in the U.S., partnering with the Rockefeller Banks, J.P. Morgan and other large national banks. They created the 'Panic of 1907' through these banks...calling in loans and tightening credit. Thousands of banks were overextended, so bank runs were common. J.P. Morgan convinced Congress that he could print up a bunch of money and give it to the branch banks, saving them from default. His plan worked and he said that what the country needed was a central bank...privately owned...with no political influence from Congress."

"Senator Nelson Aldrich, from a Rhode Island banking family, chaired a National Monetary Commission, established by Congress in 1909 to study the feasibility of a central bank that would control and stabilize the banking system of the U.S. He traveled to Europe for two years talking with the Rothschilds about how to establish a central bank in the U.S. He met and spent many hours with Paul Warburg, a wealthy German banking partner of the Rothschilds. The Rothschilds sent Warburg to the U.S. that year to establish a central bank for them. Incidentally, Nelson Aldrich's daughter married David Rockefeller, and his grandson by this marriage was Nelson Aldrich Rockefeller, former Governor of New York and Vice President of the U.S."

Amy paused for a drink and began again, "To formulate their plan for a central bank, they needed secrecy...wanted no newspaper reporters around...and these reporters followed the big bankers wherever they went, looking for a story. These money lenders knew that Congress and the public were not in favor of a central bank, one controlled by the big New York banks, so they took elaborate steps to keep any knowledge of these planning sessions from the press.

The seven bankers chosen to formulate this plan that would be submitted to Congress for approval, stealthily boarded Senator Aldrich's private railcar in the middle of the night on November 10th, 1910...one by one, at appointed times. Then they were taken down the east coast to Jekyll Island, Georgia, off the coast of Brunswick. The island was owned by J.P. Morgan, the home of a luxurious hunting club he used to entertain his wealthy friends...very private. The island would be for their exclusive use.

The regular help was excused for the week... people who would know some of the bankers who had been guests of J.P. Morgan on previous hunting trips. Replacements were brought in from the mainland. The only regular employees there that week were the manager of the club and the hunting director."

"Hey," I yelled loudly as I jumped up out of my chair. "I've heard this story...my Uncle Fed was that hunting director. My dad told me of this event when I was still in college." The others gave me a look of astonishment as I sat back down in my chair.

Kathy began again, "The seven men in attendance represented nearly 50% of the wealth in the world. Those men were:

Nelson Aldrich, U.S. Senator from Rhode Island

Abraham Piatt Andrews, Assistant Secretary of the Treasury, and

Member of the National Monetary Commission

Frank A. Vanderlip, President, National City Bank of New York

Henry Davisson, President, Liberty National Bank, Founder of Bankers Trust Group, and Partner of J.P. Morgan

Charles Norton, President, First National Bank of New York

Benjamin Strong, Vice President, Bankers Trust and J.P. Morgan Bank

Paul Warburg, Partner with Kuhn, Loeb and Company, a bank controlled by the Rothschilds.

These men agreed to not use their real names while on Jekyll Island. Each had made up a name to use for the week."

Paul Warburg, having set up several central banks for the Rothschilds in Europe was the most knowledgeable one in the group. His ideas prevailed and thus a Rothschild central bank was the outcome. The name of the bank was most important so as to not arouse suspicion and opposition from the start. They didn't want the Congress and the people to know that it is a Rothschild private banking cartel. They chose the name Federal so that people would assume it was part of the government. It's no more part of the U.S. government than Federal Express or Federal Bake Shop. The name Reserve was chosen rather than calling it a bank…System rather than a price fixing cartel that it is. The Federal Reserve System would dominate the cash reserves of banks all over the country. The FED would have a monopoly over U.S. currency… being able to create money out of thin air and then lending it to U.S. banks and to the government…even to foreign banks. It would operate with complete independence from Congress… no audit and only minimal oversight."

"A majority of Congress was against this bill establishing the Federal Reserve System," Amy said, "and they voted it down once. It finally became law on December 23, 1913 when both Houses of Congress rammed it through while enough of the bill's opponents were away on Christmas vacation. President Woodrow Wilson signed it into law immediately, giving the Rothschilds another 20-year charter. The 'money lenders' were in power once again to run their 'invisible government' scheme…against the wishes of the people and the majority of Congress. They now needed to pass an income tax law that would provide a steady stream of money to the FED to pay off the interest on the debt that was certain to accumulate. It is no coincidence that our current Federal Income Tax Law was passed that same year."

"World War I began in 1914 and it was a huge money maker for the Rothschilds. The German Rothschilds lent money to the Germans...The French Rothschilds to the French to finance their war effort...and the British Rothschilds financed the British Army. When the U.S. entered World War I, The Rothschilds and the FED were there to provide all of the money our government needed to finance the war...at a slight interest rate. The 'money lenders' would make billions off of World War I."

Kathy took over for Amy at this point. "Republican President Warren Harding was elected in 1920, inheriting a deep recession brought about by the FED's over-reaction to the post- war economic expansion. The economy was growing and the FED decided to drive it down by tightening the money supply and raising interest rates. Harding disliked the banking practices of the FED. He favored the free market rather than artificial manipulation by the Federal Reserve. President Harding took the exact opposite actions of those recommended by the FED. He cut government spending, lowered tax rates, reduced our debt to the FED, and reduced interest payments on that debt. The economy recovered much more quickly than anyone expected…a testament to our free market system."

"But remember," Kathy reminded us, "the FED is a privately owned banking cartel in business for one reason only, to make money for its stockholders. The Rothschilds were furious with Harding. They couldn't have a president who did not want to borrow money and run up government debt. Things must change. It was reported that President Harding suddenly died of food poisoning in August of 1923, though there was no autopsy."

Kathy continued, "President Calvin Coolidge took over and cut government spending even more, reduced taxes further, raised tariffs to protect our industries…grew the economy throughout the Roaring Twenties…continuing the proven performance of an economy free from too much government spending. The Rothchilds couldn't have Coolidge either. They decided in 1929 to wreck our economy and blame Coolidge."

"Throughout the Roaring Twenties farms and businesses expanded their operations to meet the demands of a good economy and were strung out on credit. Through its member banks the FED began calling in loans, tightening credit and the supply of money, causing large numbers of businesses and farms to fall into bankruptcy and foreclosure. Before the FED took these steps, however, Paul Warburg sent a secret memo to all of his wealthy friends warning them to sell all off their stocks because the market is sure to fall. When the stock market collapsed in October, 1929 these money lenders were in a cash position to buy up land, buildings and businesses of all kinds for just pennies on the dollar. Farm owners were now tenants and business men were now hunting jobs. It is estimated that 40 billion dollars was lost on that Black Monday stock market crash. But it wasn't really lost…it ended up in the hands of the money lenders."

"The Federal Reserve could have helped the economy at that time by lowering interest rates and increasing the money supply, but they did the opposite. The FED reduced the money supply by 33%, deepening and prolonging the Great Depression. The FED then transferred billions of dollars to the Central Bank of Germany, helping them to rebuild war torn Germany and finance Hitler to power," Kathy explained.

Ben stood up and stretched. "This is incredible information." he sighed. "But is this all recorded fact?"

Kathy continued, "Yes…and there is much more. History's most outspoken opponent of the FED has been Congressman Louis McFadden, who served in the House in the 1920's until the mid thirties. He conducted a 15-year investigation of the FED, uncovering much of their illegal activities with regard to transferring money out of the U.S. Treasury to support their foreign banking operations. McFadden was a relentless thorn in the FED's side, constantly calling for the repeal of their charter. Congressman McFadden died suddenly in October, 1936 of a heart attack, brought on by the 'intestinal flu,' as it was mysteriously diagnosed. Prior to his death there were two other attempts on his life. Once he became violently ill while eating at a political banquet. His life was saved by a doctor friend at the banquet who immediately got a stomach pump and gave McFadden emergency treatment. The Congressman had been poisoned. A third attempt was made on his life as he got out of a cab in front of a hotel. Three pistol shots were fired at him and hit the cab. None hit McFadden."

"Again, the Rothschilds funded both sides of World War II, adding billions more to their central bank assets. American taxpayers financed more than half of the war's total costs, leaving us heavily in debt...the money lenders made billions."

Kathy paused for a sip of her coke. "After the war, the world was divided...capitalism against communism. Now it was time for the Rothschilds to go after their goal of 'one world government', using this division. The Rothschild money lenders would surely take advantage of the arms race that followed, financing both sides of the cold war arms race...primarily between Russia and the U.S. This would be as profitable for them as a military conflict. A 'central bank for the world' was created when they formed The World Bank and The International Monetary Fund. The United Nations was established to eventually become the governing body of the Rothschilds' New World Order."

Kathy looked at everyone as she scanned the three of us. "This next point will send chills up and down your spine. President Kennedy did not like the FED. He saw it driving the stock market up and down over the years in order to make big profits for its own Wall Street investment banks...to the detriment of taxpayers and the U.S. government. In June, 1963 Kennedy signed a Presidential Order which returned to the U.S. government the power to issue currency, without going through the privately owned Federal Reserve System. The FED was now out of business...no loans to our government...no interest payments on that debt. The Treasury Department now assumed its Constitutional authority to create and issue currency. More than 4 billion dollars of President Kennedy's U.S. Notes were put into the economy before he was assassinated in November. They looked just like Federal Reserve Notes except that 'United States Note' was printed on them. President Kennedy courageously challenged the Rothschilds's central bank, the Federal Reserve System, in the two ways it profits most:

1. War....Kennedy promised to have our troops out of Viet Nam by 1965.
2. Control of the currency...His Executive Order would have destroyed the Federal Reserve."

"President Kennedy realized what a scam the FED is and took his case to the American people. Ten days before he was assassinated President Kennedy said in a speech to Columbia University, 'The high office of the presidency has been used to foment a plot to destroy America's freedom, and before I leave office, I must inform the citizen of his plight.' His assassination might have been a warning to all future U.S. Presidents not to interfere with the FED's control over the currency… it alone will create money. President Johnson immediately lifted Kennedy's Executive Order that would eliminate the FED, and the war in Viet Nam was expanded…more money for the money lenders."

As Kathy continued talking, my mind flashed back to the story that my dad told me long ago…. about Uncle Fed and Jekyll Island. Dad knew what he was talking about.

"In 1987 the Rothschilds created the World Conservation Bank. Third World countries may now transfer the debts they cannot afford to pay, to this bank in exchange for land. Third World countries held 33% of the world's land surface, and the Rothschilds wanted particular, mineral rich tracts of land located in these countries. It was a huge profit center for the Rothschilds, allowing them to now control 80% of the worlds' supply of Uranium…giving them a monopoly over nuclear energy. They own 70% of the world's gold. Their London Gold offices set the price of gold each morning, driving it up and down artificially…reaping huge profits either way."

"The Rothschilds own controlling interest in the world's top three oil companies…Shell Oil, British Petroleum and through their Rockefeller partners, Exxon oil. Now you know why oil can be purchased only with U.S. dollars on the open market. Some reliable estimates of the Rothschild families' net worth totals more than 400 trillion dollars. And here's a big one…the Rothschilds own controlling interest in all three major TV networks…ABC, NBC and CBS…so the public knows only what the 'money lenders' want them to know. They can make or break a politician in a minute… all politicians know that. They have nearly enough power for their long sought 'one world government' with ruling elites in charge. They must have a more weakened United States, however. They don't have that yet, but they are close." Kathy paused to catch her breath.

Ben stood up…hand on his chin…looking down at the floor then up to face us. "I know what we have to do now. We must work to abolish the Federal Reserve System…it's unconstitutional… its 20-year charter expired in 1933, so it's operating illegally…and it's a scam operation. It places the burden of stabilizing the world's economy squarely on the backs of American business entrepreneurs and the superior productive capacity of everyday working Americans. It's as clear as a bell, the FED has stolen the wealth that we have created, and distributed it to the rest of the world through their foreign banks. Congress has given the FED 100 years of taxpayer money and the FED has given us nothing but paper money created out of thin air."

Kathy quickly added, "They don't even print up the money anymore...just make a data entry for 300 billion dollars in the Treasury's account... with nothing to back it up but the 'promise to pay' by the U.S. government. The FED has created the illusion that real money has been made and real money has been loaned to the U.S. government, but it hasn't. The money from the FED is real only if the U.S. taxpayer makes good on it, by paying the interest and the accumulated debt. All of these years we have simply borrowed money from ourselves, and paid the FED interest on our money...money that is backed only by the earning capacity of American labor and businesses. As I see it, we don't owe the FED anything."

Amy then spoke up, "The Federal Reserve is the central bank of the U.S., privately owned by the Rothschilds and friends...with the power to issue currency. Here's what is disturbing to me...the Rothschilds now own the European Union Central Bank, the Central Banks of China, Russia and the central banks of every country in the world except three...Cuba, Iran and North Korea...with the same power to manufacture currency out of thin air. The reason the FED is so adamant that Congress cannot audit their books is that they don't want us to know how many U.S. dollars have been transferred to other banks around the world to prop up their operations when those countries get into financial trouble. You're right Ben. We must do away with the FED."

I added to the conversation, "Removing the FED could be a difficult and dangerous undertaking. The Rothschilds have worked for over 250 years to get to this point...where the elites can control the world with a 'one world government.' They control the economies of the world... the politicians and the governments. But they are not so certain that they have adequate control of the people...especially those independent, freedom loving souls in the U.S....with Tea Party attitudes. If we are going to stop them...end it right now, we can't wait. We can throw the Rothschilds out of the U.S. just as Andy Jackson did, and pay off our accumulated debt without too much trouble, simply by creating our own interest free and debt-free currency. This would set an example for other countries to follow...when they see how much better off they are without a privately owned bank controlling their currency and dictating monetary policy."

Kathy said, "Too few Congressmen are in favor of repealing the Federal Reserve Act. They fear the complications and the previous threats of the FED to bring about a financial disaster. The key to gaining more support is to expose the FED for what it is, by pushing for a bill to audit the Fed."

"That's exactly what we'll do," Ben said. "We start campaigning next week for reelection in November and I, again, will be speaking in support of my Republican colleagues in the House and Senate who expect difficult races. That means I'll be in all parts of the country with the same message...'we need to audit the Federal Reserve.' Dan, let's you and I get busy writing some speeches."

Thirteen

Ben began his message that we should audit the FED the following week while speaking for a fellow Congressman in Indiana. His passion in describing the ills of the FED took the Congressman by surprise, but he was glad Ben lent his national prominence and popularity to his re-election efforts. I informed Ben that the polls had him leading his challenger by thirty points in his own race back home. He then doubled his efforts to speak around the country on behalf of his Republican friends in the House and the Senate… speaking at 41 Republican campaign events around the country in the 93 days leading up to the November election…same message everywhere he went, "let's audit the FED."

The Republicans regained control of the House, but the Democrats held on to the Senate. Many Republican leaders told me that Ben was primarily responsible for the success they had in those hotly contested Congressional Districts... giving them control of the House. They now have the ability to stop the uncontrolled spending that a Democrat controlled House, Senate and Presidency would have allowed.

It was an exhausting campaign for Ben...hard on Kathy, Amy and me, too. The four of us had a rather quiet Thanksgiving dinner together, with no plans for Christmas. Dannie and Bennie, however, got together with the girls and planned a family week at Snowshoe Resort in West Virginia...renting a big chalet in the mountains that would house all of us. "I'm glad they included us," Amy laughed.

"Yeaaah, I guess the children are taking control of the family get-togethers now and we're just invited tag-a-longs," Kathy added jokingly.

It was a fun and restful week for us all. I'm still in awe at our family situation...so is Ben. Just the two of us sitting in front of the fireplace, he remarked, "Isn't it great that our children and grandchildren love each other so much. I mean, you and I have always been best friends and we have always wanted to be close to each other...that's all I ever wanted of our relationship. Never in my wildest dreams, however, would I have thought that Kathy and Amy would become just as close as you and I are. And you do know that the children and grandchildren call each other throughout the year in between our two traditional family vacations at Christmas and during the summer."

I looked over at him. "I never thought of our relationship being more than two childhood friends, meeting a few times a week to run or work out, spend a few minutes talking with each other about things going on in our lives...dinner with the wives occasionally. I could have settled with that kind of relationship with my best friend. I think, however, that God has a different plan for us. He wanted more from us than we could envision...and He is still unfolding His plan before us...isn't through with us yet."

"Yes, I know," Ben said, "and I can't wait to see what He has in store for us next."

Ben took his seat in the 112th Congress in January, 2011. His and other Republicans' biggest concern is that our accumulated debt has now reached 13.5 trillion dollars and growing. By the end of this fiscal year it is expected to be nearly 15 trillion dollars.. Throughout 2011 Ben joined with Congressman Ron Paul and a few other Republicans on the Monetary Oversight Committee to push for an audit of the FED. FED Chairman, Ben Bernanke, continued to warn that this kind of interference will adversely affect the political independence of the Federal Reserve... prompting it to do things which might do harm to our nation's economy. At one such time Ben asked, "Is that a warning sir?"

"No," Bernanke replied, "but the Federal Reserve contends, always, that if we are to make good monetary decisions we must be free from the political influence of outsiders, and that includes the close scrutiny of the Congress that you seem to want."

Ben responded to the Chairman, "I don't see how anyone who is working for the people of the U.S. could object to a reasonable examination of the books of the FED, so we can be certain that the people's taxes are being spent wisely." Ben was not in awe of the FED, as some of his colleagues seemed to be.

In 2012 Ben kicked up the rhetoric a bit. It was an election year and he wanted to do all that he could do to help Republicans keep the House and to regain the Senate. In August, before the fall election campaigning started, Ben spoke passionately from the floor of the House. "The FED has not lived up to its mandate of stabilizing our banking system and keeping our economy on a steady course. No, over the hundred years in which they have been in control of our economy, there have been many ups and down… even collapses of the economy, as in the Great Depression. They either don't know what they are doing or they are deliberately manipulating our economy for the private gain of their foreign stockholders. The FED will gladly comply with Congress's increasing appetite for money…printing up all that we ask for. Shame on us, for we are also to blame for running up this huge mountain of debt. Many of you have said, 'Debt doesn't matter…just keep printing money.' Well, I'm here to say that is a foolish idea. It will bring our great nation to ruin. The American taxpayer is paying the FED hundreds of billions of dollars each year in interest payments, and that is morally wrong. We need more details of just exactly how the FED has conducted bank rescues…and an open book on the FED's support of foreign central banks. My fellow Congressmen, we need to audit the Federal Reserve System."

Ben received a standing ovation from the right side of the aisle…not much response from the Democrat left side.

In the fall of 2012, our polls showed that Ben was assured of re-election, so he again set out to assist in the campaigns of his friends in the House and the Senate. Mitt Romney had not asked for Ben's help in his bid for the Presidency because they concluded that Romney would carry Tennessee anyway. Ben and I questioned some of Romney's campaign leaders about some of their strategy, but they didn't seem to want any help from us. Ben went to every section of the country speaking on behalf of his friends who were up for re-election and for a few newcomers running for the first time. He drew large crowds everywhere he went. His popularity was astonishing. When speaking about the ills of the FED, the fervor of his delivery produced a sound much like that of preacher on Sunday morning…the people standing, shouting and applauding wildly. They loved Ben…he delivered.

Ben was constantly asked by Fox News to comment on a variety of situations. He was sought after by many conservative radio talk show hosts, but the major networks and CNN no longer wanted him on the air. His comments and speech excerpts were never in the liberal newspapers either. We discussed it and I was certain that the Rothschilds put out the word that he was not to be given a platform to speak on any of the main stream TV networks or newspapers they controlled. They wanted him silenced.

Ben and Kathy walked down the hall to have breakfast with Amy and me on the morning after the election and talk over the election results around the country. Ben won re-election by a large majority…no surprise. What was a bit surprising, though, is that he got 23% of the black vote… happy about that…making progress in changing minds. He was disappointed with the results in a few of the races in which he campaigned hard for his friends who lost. The GOP retained control of the House but the Senate remained in Democrat hands.

The four of us agreed to have a quiet Thanksgiving dinner together again this year. The kids got together and planned for a Christmas at home…in Chattanooga…haven't done that in a while. Neva and Anna had our home beautifully decked out with all of our old traditional decorations when we got there...brought a tear to Amy's eyes when she saw them. Sarah had done the same for Ben and Kathy's house. Amy and Kathy shopped every day during the five days before Christmas...gifts for all of the grandchildren...from each side of the family.

All twenty-two of us met for dinner at Ben and Kathy's house on Christmas Eve and exchanged gifts that evening. We didn't go to Gatlinburg between Christmas and New Years Day as we have done so often in the past. This year the children decided that they wanted to stay around Chattanooga, look up old friends and hang out together. In Amy and Kathy's case, return gifts that needed to be exchanged and shop the after-Christmas sales at the malls. Each evening we were either at Ben and Kathy's house or ours... eating and sitting around the fire...talking about old times together as a family...where should we go on summer vacation this year. Ben and I just looked at each other and smiled, filled with pride at what our families had become.

Ben and I got right to work as the 113th U.S. Congress began in January, 2013. The House finally passed a bill to audit the Federal Reserve. It was written by Congressman Ron Paul. I don't think the bill has much of a chance to pass in the Senate. Ben and I began working with other Republicans to develop strategies to regain control of the Senate. This is crucial in the 2014 elections if we are to move forward with our efforts to audit the FED and ultimately abolish it. We must identify key Senate races and get the right people to run for those seats... and then give them all of the support they need.

Throughout 2013 Ben kept busy on the speaker's circuit, relentlessly pounding the Federal Reserve at a variety of events...Tea Party Meetings, graduations, business and trade conventions and political fundraisers. In 2013 Ben would raise more money for the Republican National Committee than anyone in the party's history. At every event he asked them to join with him and other Republicans in Congress to pass legislation requiring an audit of the FED, an audit which he knew would bring about a demand that the FED be abolished. The FED knew it, too. Ben was driven by the urgency to get our spending and debt under control. The accumulated debt is expected to reach 17.5 trillion dollars by the end of 2013 and 19 trillion dollars at the end of 2014... astronomical figures...must be stopped.

As 2014 elections neared, Ben and I picked nine Senate races that we thought could be won by a Republican...Senate seats now held by Democrats. Six of the Senate Republican candidates welcomed Ben's offer to help in their campaign. Three of them made it clear that they didn't want Ben interfering in their campaigns. He visited each state four or five times, speaking for the candidates...convincing voters that their candidate was needed in the Senate. Ben was successful. Five of the contests were won by Republicans, enough to give them control of the Senate. Ben let it be known that he and other Republicans now had the power to pass legislation in both Houses of Congress to audit the Federal Reserve...exactly what he would do when the new Senators are sworn into office in January.

We were all happy with the election results... decided to take Kathy and Amy out for dinner two nights later to celebrate...just a nice little quiet place on a side street...nothing real fancy... one of our favorite places to eat. We savored the food and the moment, a nice feeling of accomplishment. After dinner while I took care of the bill, Ben and girls went outside to hail a cab. As I turned to leave, I heard multiple gunshots ring out. Hurrying outside, I was horrified to see Ben and Kathy lying on the sidewalk, each with blood spilling out of several wounds...not moving at all. Amy was sitting up on the sidewalk...beside them screaming, crying...looking down at Ben and Kathy, "No, No, No," was all she could cry out... blood running down her arm from a shoulder wound. Someone from the restaurant was calling for an ambulance as I bent over Kathy's body... three massive bullet wounds in the chest...no chance...Kathy was dead. Ben was breathing but unconscious...not moving. Amy was hit in her left shoulder, losing lots of blood.

Three hours later at the hospital I was sitting next to Amy's hospital bed when a doctor came in and told me that Kathy was dead and that Ben was paralyzed from the waist down… would never walk again. Amy was asleep on pain medication… couldn't hear me cry. "How…why, God, could this happen?" I wept next to her bed all night long.

Amy awakened the following morning and asked me what happened. I told her and she wept bitterly for a few minutes. "Does Ben know?" she asked.

"No, he is still asleep…thought I'd let the doctors tell him…he'll have lots of questions when he wakes up."

I told Amy that I had called all of the children and that Dannie and Sarah would be here tomorrow to see Ben. Late that afternoon, police investigators came to the hospital and talked to Amy about the crime. She told them that a car stopped on the narrow side street in front of the restaurant. She was talking with Ben and Kathy… not looking at the car, but she knew that it was there. Then the shots…she was hit and knocked down by the force of the bullet…eyes glued to Ben and Kathy as they took multiple hits. She never got a look at the car. Ben would later tell the investigators the same story. He didn't pay attention to the car and no one has come forward to give a description of the vehicle. There would never be any clue as to who did this evil deed.

Six days later Kathy's body was flown back to Chattanooga for burial in their family plot. A Congressman friend of Ben's offered to have Ben, Amy and me flown back to Chattanooga in his private jet. Doctors didn't want Ben to go but he went anyway. We made him comfortable with pillows and blankets piled around him. The funeral service was a wonderful tribute to Kathy. Dannie took over from me and pushed Ben's wheelchair into the church, down front next to Kathy's casket.

Business friends spoke of Kathy's generous heart, always giving to others in need. The owner of her accounting firm said emphatically, as he spoke of her ability, "Kathy could have been anything she wanted to be...president of a major corporation or even President of the United States...she was that smart. But she chose to love God...her husband...her family...her friends...to love those in need. That was the priority of her life and she never waivered from that in the 35 years that I knew her." Ben smiled at those comments...he knew that.

We remained in Chattanooga for a week, giving Ben and Amy more time to heal. Amy and I stayed with Neva and her children at our house and Ben stayed with Sarah and her family at his house. I rented a handicap van and every day I picked Ben up and took him to the cemetery where he would visit with Kathy for more than an hour...mourning her deeply...broke my heart to see it. We would have lunch together but he ate very little…talked very little.

On Sunday afternoon after our visit to Kathy's gravesite, Ben said to me, "See if you can arrange to get that plane back here in Chattanooga and fly us back to Washington. We have some work to get done."

Three days later we were back in Washington. "I'm gonna hire someone to assist me in my condo…cook, keep the place clean, help me get dressed each day…do anything I need in my place. But I want you to push my wheelchair to work each day. Everywhere I go, I want you with me…to be not only my legs, but my eyes and ears, too. Can you do that, Dan?"

"Yes, Ben," I replied. "You know that I can and will do that."

Two weeks later I loaded Ben into his specially equipped van and drove to the Capitol for his first day back since the shooting. I pushed his wheelchair through the Capitol Rotunda and later into the long hallway leading to the House chamber. I was surprised to see the hall lined on both sides with members of Congress and their staff personnel. As I moved the wheelchair forward they began to clap their hands, slowly at first. Ben looked up at me and yelled over the noise, "Run, Dan." I didn't know what he wanted so I broke into a slow jog and they began to clap louder. "No, run, run, run," he yelled even louder. I began to jog at a brisk pace but Ben yelled even louder over the increasing noise from the bystanders. "Faster, faster, faster!" he yelled whirling his arm around as if cracking a whip, now flashing that "Big Ben Grin." Although he was safely strapped in his wheelchair, I thought we were acting a bit dangerously, so I slowed down as we entered through the open doors of the House Chamber.

I pushed Ben down to a prepared place for him at the front row of seats. Several of his colleagues welcomed him back, taking turns at the microphone, offering condolences for his losses. Then Ben spoke to the House, "Mr. Speaker and fellow Representatives, thank you for that warm welcome and the expressions of sympathy. I won't take up all of my allotted time, but I do want to speak to you for a few minutes about the work that I feel we must do…audit the Federal Reserve System. For over a hundred years the FED has been granted by Congress the right to run our economy…with their stated goal of stabilizing the economy and preventing inflation. We have illegally allowed them to set interest rates, to create the currency of the United States government and to set the amount of money in circulation. The Constitution gives that responsibility to the Congress only. The FED's charter expired in 1933, so they have operated over eighty years with no legal authority to do so."

"The Federal Reserve is a private banking corporation, whose primary goal is the same as in every private enterprise…to make money for its stockholders. It is the central bank of U.S. with twelve branch banks around the country. Its top priority is not to look out for the well being of the American taxpayers, but to make money for its foreign owners. That's why we have seen a continuous run of wide swings in the economy during the past 100 years in which they have been in control of the economy. It's why we have seen growing inflation that has eroded the value of our dollar.

The FED's stockholders and associated Wall Street Bankers make a lot of money when the stock market goes up and a lot of money when it goes down, unlike most of us who don't have insider information. It is profitable for them to manipulate the economy up and down by raising and lowering interest rates...by printing up more dollars and expanding the money supply...calling in loans and contracting the money supply. It is not profitable for the American taxpayers who need a more stable economy in order to plan for their individual needs.

The FED's ownership is made up primarily of a few elite, extremely wealthy European bankers and a few closely associated U.S. bankers. An audit of the Federal Reserve System will show their close connection. They are elitists who believe that the world would be much better off if they ruled it...making all of the decisions for the weak and ignorant masses of people... erasing boundaries between countries and, thereby, eliminating nationalism and war. They would exert their will over that of each unknowledgeable individual. This will eliminate poverty and disease and create a utopian society of 'one world government'.

This close knit group of 30-40 individuals controls nearly half of the world's wealth. They not only own the FED and rule our politicians, they own similarly run central banks in every country in the world except Cuba, Iran and North Korea. An audit of the FED will reveal that they have secretly moved trillions of our dollars to the central banks of other countries around the world. These foreign central banks then lend these dollars to private banks within their country which need more money to cover bad loans they have made. These troubled banks are owned by this group of money lenders. It is the biggest scam in history… making the U.S. taxpayer support the financial stability of the whole world…bailing out greedy bankers around the world who have made risky loans. Shame on us, my friends in the Congress, for allowing that to happen. This group of elite money lenders has stolen trillions of dollars of our country's wealth and we have let them get away with it for a hundred years."

Ben looked around the chamber, gazing at both sides of the aisle. "We, in Congress, are planning to borrow over a trillion dollars this year from the Federal Reserve by selling to them Treasury Bonds that we print up. The FED doesn't have a trillion dollars in their vaults, so they just crank up the money presses and print up one trillion dollars and deposit the money into the account of the U.S. Treasury. These days the FED doesn't even bother to print up the dollars. They just make an electronic data entry into the Treasury's account. With the stroke of a key, we Congressmen now have one trillion dollars to spend. Can it get any easier than this? The FED just created one trillion dollars out of thin air and loaned it to us."

Ben paused and then said, "We're no longer on the gold standard so what is backing up the one trillion dollars that has just been deposited into our account by the FED?" Seeming to wait for an answer, Ben slowly scanned the faces of those in the chamber. "That money is backed up only by the 'promise to pay' by the U.S. government… 'the full faith and trust' of the U.S. government. Now, our government's only way to get money is to tax the people and businesses. So it is the taxpayer and the entrepreneur who stands behind the debt that we keep running up… they are the ones who back up the money created by the FED." So, you see, it's not the FED's money that our government borrowed…it's our money. We borrowed it from ourselves…and we paid interest on <u>our</u> money…not the FED's money. It is foolish to think that we have borrowed money from ourselves and that we have to repay that money to someone else…with interest."

Ben continued, "By abolishing the FED we can wipe out most of the 19 trillion dollars in debt. We begin by doing the same thing Andrew Jackson, Abraham Lincoln and John Kennedy did as president…we print up all of our own currency…replace all Federal Reserve Notes with U.S. Notes… seize all U.S. assets held by the FED…assure all private banks in the U.S. and abroad that their reserves will be protected as always…and guarantee the soundness of the U.S. dollar to the rest of the world. Doing this will allow us to reduce taxes, reach full employment, shore up Social Security funds and help keep inflation in check. The elite money lenders will fight it…claim that this will cause a worldwide panic and cause governments to fall. We must work with other countries who want to do the same with their central banks. This will be a difficult and dangerous thing to do, but it is something that we must do if we are going to get out of this terrible mess."

Ben again paused, looked around the room and added, "God created us with a 'free will.' We can choose to obey God or not to obey Him. This desire for freedom is a gift from God that is the essence of our being. Our Creator hasn't taken it away from us…we can still choose to rebel against God. That's how important our free will is to the One who made us…that He would allow us to turn our backs on Him and rebel against Him, rather than coerce us into submission to His will. If the elite money lenders have their way and succeed in bringing about a 'one world government,' they would exert their will over the individual's will…

something even God hasn't done. It is immoral for us to continue this way. We must take back our Constitutional authority to control the monetary policy of the United States. We must abolish the Federal Reserve System. It is the moral thing to do." Ben received a thunderous applause from both sides of the aisle as I pushed him back to his spot on the floor.

Congressman Ron Paul reintroduced his bill to audit the FED and the House passed it overwhelmingly. The new Republican Senate passed a similar bill introduced by Senator Rand Paul in early February, 2015.

Now it was up to President Obama to sign the bill and make it law...would he do it? The President requested a meeting of Ben and other Congressmen who sponsored the bill. I pushed Ben into the White House and we joined the others in his conference room. There was much discussion between the President and everyone in attendance about our country's monetary policy. His economic advisors were especially vocal on a variety of details, arguing for the FED. President Obama said that he agreed with Ben's opinion that to continue our monetary policy as it is would be unfair and even immoral to the American people. The President wasn't convinced that it was the thing to do at this time, however. His concern was the potential for worldwide economic chaos that could occur if the world's banking elite fought back hard... manipulating the monetary policies of the various countries that they still controlled, in ways that would do us harm.

Ben spoke up for the second time during the meeting. "I know this bunch…know that they will fight back. We cannot be afraid of what they might do. We must do what is right for our people. If we continue to go down this reckless path of excessive spending it will destroy this great idea for freedom that our founding fathers came up with. Congress has allowed this scam of the Federal Reserve to go on long enough. History will judge this Congress harshly if we allow the FED to continue operating…and Mr. President, if you don't sign this act of Congress to abolish the FED, history will also judge you accordingly." The President didn't respond verbally, but his facial expressions told me that he was not pleased with Ben's prediction.

Nine weeks later, April 12, 2015, President Obama signed the bill calling for an audit of the FED. "We did it," Ben said while folding up his newspaper and reaching for a cup of coffee. He was finishing breakfast as I came into his condo from down the hall where I had just had my breakfast, one of Amy's world-famous ham and cheese omelets. The headline on the newspaper read, 'President Signs FED Audit Bill."

"Now the real work begins," I replied.

"I'm way ahead of you," Ben said. "The Europeans, the Chinese and the Russians have assured us that they will join us in abolishing their central banks, all owned by the Rothschild family and friends. We made it easy for them to see the scam that was going on, so they and other countries have booted the Rothschilds out of their countries, too. So far the money lenders have taken no action to indicate that they are willing to fight all of us to hang on to their money making fraud."

I responded to his comment, "Maybe they will resort to making an honest living now. They certainly have the means to do so."

Ben thought for a moment, "No…I don't think they will give up the idea of one day ruling the world. They are patient…been working this scheme for over 250 years. No…I think they'll just lie low for a while to see what happens. Like they did when President Andrew Jackson drove them out, they'll wait for an opportunity to occur. The elite 'money lenders' will do as they have in the past…wait for a new generation to come along which won't be so diligent in monitoring history…easily swayed by their promises. They won't give up…they'll be back. Remember, they still control the largest banks in the world and most of the world's energy and precious resources, so we need to watch them closely."

Ben took his last sip of coffee and set his cup down. "How would you like to go for a stroll outside…get a little fresh air?" I asked.

"Sounds wonderful to me," Ben said. I grabbed the handles of his wheel chair and began pushing it down the hall of our condo building... out across the street to the sidewalks along the Potomac...inhaling the aroma of the cherry tree blossoms...taking in the view along the grassy banks of the river.

"Walk beside me," Ben said. "Let me push my wheels." I did as he asked, walking beside him, watching him move his arms in perfect rhythm... powerful strokes now turning those wheels. He had been practicing...pushing faster now...had to jog to keep up with him. Ben then looked up at me with that "Big Ben Grin." "Faster," he said as he picked up speed and left me behind, pulling away from me. Looking over his shoulder, I heard him yell, laughingly, "You know that you could never run as fast as I could!"

References

John P. Curran, "JFK vs. The Federal Reserve", rense.com, April 19, 2007

Joyce Cox, "Federal Reserve Power", Wikipedia Link

Gary North, "How To End The Federal Reserve System", Lewrockwell.com

Michael Snyder, "10 Things that Everyone Should Know About the FED", theeconomiccollapseblog.com

Kyle Prast, "Happy Birthday America", Brookfield7.com, July 3, 2006

G. Edward Griffin, "The Creature From Jekyll Island", November 30, 2010

"Hearings On Monetary Policy and State of the Economy", Hearings/House Committee on Financial Services

"The Council on Foreign Relations and the New World Order", conspiracyarchive.com

www.iamthe witness.com, "History of the House of Rothschild", Andrew Hitchcock

Running... To Save America
ABOUT THE AUTHOR

DON FLANDERS

DON FLANDERS grew up in Garden City, a suburb of Savannah, Georgia, in the late forties, fifties and sixties. He received his BBA degree from the University of Georgia in 1965. Don worked for thirty years in the advertising agency business, specializing in new car dealerships.

He is a Certified Lay Speaker in the Holston Conference of the United Methodist Church. His love of God, family, sports, history, politics and his country led him to write his first novel.